A.N. PAYTON

Steams and Screams

Edited by The Assist, LLC.

Cover by GetCovers

Trigger Warning: This book may contain sensitive topics such as murder, loss, violence, or other triggers. Please be aware of your limit as a reader.

First edition

This book was professionally typeset on Reedsy.
Find out more at reedsy.com

Contents

Hallow's Promise

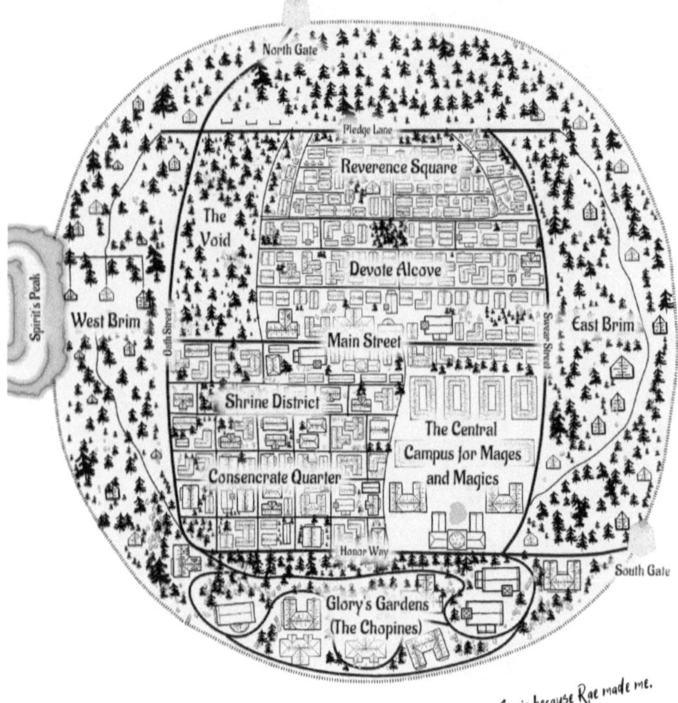

Chapter 1

Another heavy sigh slipped through my lips. This time, my hand didn't shake as I passed the customer their tea through the open window in the side of my traveling potion wagon—Brew-Tea-Ful. That was an improvement, I decided. The entire day was better than yesterday, which had been better than the day before.

Better—not great.

The customer outside the wagon cradled his tea in both hands. Steam scented with ginger and mint rose from the red tea base sourced from the desert region to the far south. Luckily, I hadn't crossed the barren hills myself. Passing traders from the market sold me the herbs several weeks ago. The slightly acidic leaves complimented the magic for my soothing potion well.

The customer took a sip, and a smile crested his lips.

Normally, the sight made my chest warm with joy. Bringing people happiness, no matter how small, reminded me of all the wonderful, simple goodness in life.

But today, I sighed.

"How long do you think it's going to take?" Krissa, my best friend, perched on a little stool in the back of the wagon, asked. She held a thick volume in both hands. I'd peeked at the pages earlier, and they were filled with numbers instead of words. It made me crunch my nose. She shifted the heavy tome, unable to rest it across her lap due to the mythical Nightingale-turned-hoglet sprawled there.

I blinked. "How long is what going to take?"

She balanced the book in one hand and waved the other in my general direction. "This. All the sighing and moping and staring sadly out the window. How much longer do I have to put up with it?"

I ground my teeth and turned away from her. "Until I feel better."

It was Krissa's turn to sigh. She set the book on the floor of the wagon with a thump, and Brew vibrated in response. Krissa wasn't the only one cross with my mood lately. Brew made its displeasure known as well.

She put her hand on my shoulder. I tensed beneath the contact. All my emotions were coiled into a tight ball in the center of my chest. If her casual touch severed a single string, the entire thing would explode.

"I'm sorry," she said.

Damn. Those words inched awfully close to one of those strings.

"I'm sorry Valen promised you the truth, and then he never showed up. I'm sorry someone you cared about lied and vanished without a word. He's the worst, and in my opinion—which I know you're not asking for, but as your best friend I'm obligated to provide—he's always been the worst."

And there it was. The reality I didn't want to think about.

Valen had lied to me. He'd promised to explain my role in his life, the future he envisioned for us, and I was going to admit my secret past and powers. We had arranged a meeting for just the two of us.

He hadn't shown up.

I had waited in The Void. Its shadows had wrapped around me like a chilled, sorrowful blanket. The beasts of that ancient part of the forest had avoided the area as though my bitterness may have been contagious. After hours in the icy snow, I'd finally walked home, only to return the next night, and the next. Valen never came.

Krissa cut right through the wispy threads keeping me together. The ball dropped like a hard stone into my gut. The other strings unwound from the spool, throwing loops of pain, rejection, anger, and everything else into my soul.

I gasped, which came out as a sob. Tears pooled in my eyes— even as I tried to stop them. To cry for the mercenary felt like a betrayal to myself.

Krissa's face twisted. She pulled me into her arms and hugged them tight around me. The pressure felt good, like she held some part of me together. Her hands wound through my hair.

"You can cry, Rae. You can't be strong all the time."

Her voice soothed some of the loose threads. "I thought he was different," I whispered into her shoulder. My tears stained the rainbow garment wrapped around her. "I thought I could trust him."

It was so hard for me to trust anyone. I'd learned that trust meant loss. Leave it to the mercenary to prove me right—*again*.

"It's so hard for you to trust. The pain is sharper when someone breaks that now." Krissa spoke the words straight from my mind. "Just because I know you're better off without him doesn't mean his absence can't hurt. You're allowed to feel however you feel."

I sniffled again as a new swell of tears burned my eyes.

Muffled voices filtered in from outside. They steadily rose until a loud shout made Krissa glance out the open window.

She straightened against me, suddenly tense.

I lifted my head and tried to see through the tears blurring my vision. I roughly brushed them away and squinted into the warming winter sun.

A stream of light fell from the sky. It went completely vertical with smooth, even edges and a uniform golden expanse. The bottom met the ground with a gentle, billowing kiss. People around the wagon seemed torn between fleeing—probably the wise choice—and staring at the beam with gaping mouths.

I pulled away from Krissa's grasp. We both huddled close to the window and looked at the smear of amber in the sky.

"What is that?" Krissa asked.

I shook my head. "No idea." Even Brew bounced from side to side, as though expressing its uncertainty as well. "We should probably leave." I doubted a big beam of light from the sky spelled anything except for trouble.

But Krissa leaned forward. Twirls of rainbow ribbons through her hair mixed color into the warm glow across her face.

She squinted. "I think there's something *inside* the light."

Sure enough, the shadowy outline of a figure darkened inside the beam. Bit by bit, the pieces solidified into a humanoid shape.

"Do you think it's from another dimension? Like how Whiskers can open voids somewhere else?"

I chewed my lip and glanced at the hoglet, now curled on the stool Krissa had abandoned. "No, I don't think it's what a Nightingale can do. It looks spellcraft-y."

"A witch?"

I shook my head. My own experience with other witches occurred under very dire circumstances at the expense of my freedom and from books I stole from the library. It had been a different time, then. I returned all my library books now.

The figure inside the light finished solidifying into a real person. Blue sky reemerged through the golden beam as it slowly faded away—leaving its deposit on the street in front of the wagon.

"Woah," Krissa said, her voice low.

Woah was right. It was a woman, adorned in layers of armor. The metal had once been carefully pieced together with gold and silver slabs. Remnants of detailed engravings etched into the pieces. At one time, this armor was pristine and glorious, prepared to order thousands of troops into battle.

But not anymore. Dents and divots cut into the panels where they'd served their purpose of defending the wearer. Debris filled the engravings in some areas or was worn too thin to see in others. Stains, looking an awful lot like blood, clung in the seam of the hinges. This armor had succumbed to the realities of war and walked side by side with its comrades toward a certain, inevitable death.

And the woman wearing it was beautiful. Ropes of blonde braids wrapped through her hair, twisting it away from her face. She didn't have a helmet to hide her fierce cheekbones or her dainty, pointed chin. In fact, covering a face like that was certainly some kind of crime to humanity.

She studied her surroundings. Most people had decided the beautiful, armored woman wasn't searching for them specifically and lingered near the perimeter of the woods to see what happened next. Her gaze cast right over them and moved on.

She was looking for something.

"Have you ever seen anyone more *beautiful*?" Krissa's voice sounded light enough that a slight breeze may blow it away.

"No," I answered, honestly.

Despite the distance across the road, and that no human could hear our hushed whispers, the woman turned to face us directly. Her eyes narrowed, and a firm, determined expression tightened her features.

I blinked. No . . .

She stepped forward, straight toward Brew, one hand palming an absolutely monstrous sword hilt on her belt.

She was looking for us.

Of course, the beautiful woman delivered from a beam of light with well-used armor and a big sword was looking for *us*. Only naivety had prevented me from realizing that right away.

"Brew." I retreated inside the small space, dragging Krissa's drooling mouth with me, until our backs hit the wall. "We need to get out of here."

Heavy stomps sounded from outside. The wagon vibrated, preparing to channel the magic in the ley-line beneath the ground to travel somewhere—anywhere—else.

Come on, come on.

An armored glove smacked against the sash. Krissa screamed and ducked into me.

Too late. If Brew traveled now, the uninvited guest would come with us. I pulled my sword from its sheath and patted the wagon's wooden wall in a silent direction to stop trying to leave. It buzzed around me, feeding off my emotions.

The woman's other hand settled on the sash, her blade taking up most of the space on the wood. I glanced at the weapon in my hand and swallowed hard. They weren't even comparable.

She would skewer me alive.

In a single, effortless motion, she hopped through the window and landed delicately on both feet inside Brew.

I sucked in a breath, brandishing my sword in middle-guard—which was more difficult with Krissa trying to hide behind me. A flash of annoyance cut through the adrenaline. I'd been planning to ward that window and having a stranger jump through it was the last straw. First thing tomorrow, the wards were going up.

If we lived that long.

Chapter 2

The woman straightened and studied my wagon. Her gaze lingered on the remnants of the tea I'd been serving, before brushing over me and Krissa against the wall.

She either didn't see my sword, or she didn't care because she stepped closer.

"My brother has gone missing. I am searching for him."

I blinked. Her voice was as crisp and clear as the koi ponds on the college campus. But also, she'd arrived from a beam of light and jumped through my window . . . to ask me to do my job? As Hallow's Promise's Crime Investigation Expert, I solved a plethora of random crimes, including murders, but my orders usually came from the town's marshal.

Krissa cleared her throat. "Have you tried talking to the marshal at the Sheriff's Station? Most people start there first . . ." Before holding someone at sword point.

The woman's eyes flashed. "The Sheriff cannot know of my presence in this place."

I leaned around her to peer out the sash, where a giant beam of light had speared the sky moments ago. I looked back at her.

She had the decency to flinch. "Yes, it wasn't the most subtle form of travel, but it was necessary. Hopefully, we will be elsewhere when authorities arrive to investigate."

I didn't have time to ponder where she planned on going, or that *I* was probably who the authorities would send to investigate. The stranger stepped forward, and I thrust the sword into her space as a warning.

But she paused. Anger flashed through her eyes first, but then they fixed upon my blade.

"Who gave you that?" she asked softly. She moved as though to stroke the sword with her fingertips, but I pulled it away.

"It doesn't matter," I ground out. Even saying his name sent pulses of anger and disappointment through me. I'd been avoiding it.

She looked at me—really looked. "I think you are the one I'm searching for."

"That makes sense," Krissa said. "She's the Crime Investigation Expert, so if someone is missing, it's her job to find them."

I was tired. Valen had stood me up. A stranger was now threatening me . . . or hiring me? It was hard to tell. But I didn't want to be part of any of it.

"Whoever you are, you need to leave this wagon. Go to the Sheriff's Station or look for your brother yourself. But leave us alone."

She jutted her perfect chin out and a coil of braids fell from her hair to wrap carefully around her neck. The armor rattled as her chest thrust forward. She could have been a painting in a castle, high above a mantel, for all to see and awe at while whispering about the strength of the woman inside the armor.

"I am Death. General of the Heretic Army. The Phoenix Queen re-risen. I alone lead the rebellion against the King of Erline, and I alone shall severe his head before the war is won." Her chest fell. The pride slipped from her face, leaving behind a lovely, also tired and sad, woman. "But before that, I was Ilene Fellentether, sister to Valen Fellentether. It is that title which brings me here. My brother Valen is missing."

My mind froze at the name, *his* name. It broke and a thousand shards shattered in my head.

"Oh." Krissa squeezed my arm. "That's why he never showed up at The Void. He didn't ignore you, Rae, he's gone *missing*."

Bile climbed up my throat. After everything Valen had promised me, I assumed the worst of him when he didn't arrive at our meeting. It made me feel sick.

But this wasn't about me at all.

Valen was involved in many dangerous endeavors. His work as a mercenary put him directly in the path of danger, but he also partook in the undertakings of Ilene's rebellion. The less upstanding members of Hallow's Promise called him the Nightwrath. If he'd gone missing, and his sister didn't know where he was, something terrible must have happened.

He could be dead.

The thought brought a flood of panic I couldn't afford, and I choked it down. Finding Valen relied on me staying calm and logical.

"How do you know he's missing?" I asked. There, a perfectly logical question.

"He hasn't answered any of my scrying attempts. It's not uncommon for us to miss one or two, but he's missed over a dozen."

My brows rose, but Krissa asked the question. "What's scrying?"

Ilene blinked. "You don't scry?" We shook our heads in unison. "It's a way to talk across distances. I'll show you. Do you have any wine? Not the good stuff, just any bottle lying around."

I bit my lip. Brew shuttered, which pushed Ilene forward, closer to me. I could either put the sword away or risk stabbing her with Brew's next temper tantrum. A sigh slipped through my lips. Realistically, Ilene would win any fight against me. Keeping the sword out was silly.

"Here, why don't you sit down while I look for the wine?" I gestured to the stool Krissa had abandoned. Whiskers lifted his head, a sleepy expression across his pointed face. Whatever the Nightingale felt in the room was enough to rouse him from the stool, and he slowly sauntered into the lower cupboard where Bubbles the warplog slept. Bubbles grunted in displeasure without bothering to open even one eye as the hoglet settled against his frog-like skin.

Ilene looked relieved as she sank onto the stool. It was a bit ridiculous watching her sit on the tiny chair. In no way was she a small woman, and the seat groaned as it threatened to buckle beneath the weight of her armor. But she looked too dazed to realize the threat of collapse coming from her perch.

"Krissa, could you shut the sash?" Now that Ilene sat, Krissa stopped cowering behind me and watched the woman with a blank expression and her mouth half open. She jerked her head at the sound of her own name, frowning at me. I raised my brows. "The sash?"

"Oh." She launched forward and pulled the wooden shutter down. The sunlight filtered into a dim glow and any curious eyes were cut from view.

I turned to the other side of the wagon in a quest for the wine Ilene requested. But my heart refused to beat the right way. I couldn't control the constant spiraling in my mind.

Valen hadn't abandoned me. Something terrible had happened, and he'd been forced to miss our meeting.

My head swam, and I clutched the countertop. My chest felt too tight. I needed . . .

The upper cabinet swung open on its own, revealing an old bottle of red wine. I knew that bottle had previously been shoved into the corner depths of the shelf, but Brew had shuffled it to the front.

Right. The wagon reminded me that I didn't have time to break down. If—no, *when*—we found Valen, I could cry and scream and succumb to the self-hatred sprouting from my heart. Until then, I needed the wine.

When I turned, Ilene had produced a large cup from *somewhere* and softly cradled it in both hands. The cork released from the glass neck of the bottle, and she offered the cup up. I dumped the wine in, pouring more than I'd expected.

"Thank you." She lowered the filled cup onto her lap and ducked her blonde head over the top of it.

Power stirred through the wagon. It wasn't as heavy as my own power, or as chilling as Valen's flavor of magic. Ilene's felt more subtle, as soft as a spring breeze across my skin. It billowed her scent around the wagon, filling the space with honeysuckle and cream. Krissa sucked in an audible gasp beside me.

All of that lovely magic oozed around the cup in Ilene's hands. The wine accepted the power like a hungry flame, eating as much as Ilene offered. A small ripple shred through the surface. Ilene stilled.

My heart thundered. Krissa and I leaned closer to the rim of the cup. We all watched, waiting for Valen's familiar shape to surface through the wine, for him to say this had been a misunderstanding.

I held my breath.

The ripples faded. Ilene's magic fell as swiftly as her expression. She allowed herself a second, maybe two, of utter despair across her features, before they smoothed into the face of a warlord once again.

She stood and dumped the wine into the inset basin in Brew's counter.

"It turns to vinegar after the magic." Were her only words.

"How would Valen know you tried to reach him this way?"

"He has the same goblet as I do. When the scrying spell begins, the cup releases a rather annoying, screeching sound. Trust me, if he were near the goblet, he would not miss my attempts."

Krissa pressed her hand against my arm. "We can't stay here. There were a lot of people that saw Ilene's . . . arrival. I'm sure word has gotten to the Sheriff's Station by now."

She was right, of course. If Leof found me with the leader of a rebel army, he'd be forced to report that to the Sheriff, who responded directly to the capital—Erline. If the king had any reason to visit Hallow's Promise, my feeble cover would be blown. Although, I'd done a perfectly good job of compromising my cover all by myself. It turned out that trusting people and making best friends meant risking my darkest secrets.

"We need to start searching for Valen right away." My knees trembled. I wanted to sink into another chair, but Ilene's width prevented me from reaching the other stool. The woman shifted in the seat, apparently unburdened by the weight of the metal panels covering her body. "Do you know where he lives?"

"Of course not." Ilene shook her head, that one golden braid wrapping around her neck like a snake. Or a noose—one that would surely find its way around my neck if the king found me. "We keep our personal information to a minimum in case either of us are captured and tortured."

The word was enough to make my stomach curl.

"You've been there, Rae," Krissa stated. "When he healed you up from the Shadow-Beasts. Don't you remember where he lives?"

I bit my lip. "I was unconscious when he took me there, and sort of passed out when we left. I only saw the inside of one room."

Ilene's brow rose. "Sort of passed out?"

"Valen may have drugged her." Krissa shrugged.

There was no '*may have*' about it. The mercenary had smiled with glee when he admitted the tea he'd given me was laced with a sedative. I don't know how we'd gotten in and out of his house, but I remembered the silken sheets comforting my wounded body. That his touch had been feather-light against my skin. I bunched my fingers into a tight fist. I would find Valen. I vowed it to myself.

"I guess that doesn't help, then." Krissa tapped her finger against her chin. "Would *anyone* know where Valen lives? I always figured he's like mist, you know. Sometimes he just disappears."

I blinked. There was one person that had been to Valen's house—of her own free will. Officially, the woman was dead. Unofficially, she ran messages through the darker parts of Hallow's Promise for the rebellion. Her attempted murder, and subsequent cover-up, made her illicit activities even easier now.

An uncomfortable bubble gurgled in my gut. I'd never told

Krissa that Adora was actually alive. I kept very few secrets from my best friend, but this wasn't my secret to tell.

Still, she would be very upset.

"There's one person that knows where Valen lives," I said, slowly. My friend's eyes widened. I glanced away from her face, guilty. "But we need someone from the Siren's Sorrow to give her the message."

"Who is it?" Krissa's voice sounded hard, cold. The swell of guilt rose again.

I sucked in a breath.

"Adora Mistgrove Bolivar."

Chapter 3

Hallow's Promise had started as a tiny village that grew faster than anticipated. Once the Central Campus for Mages and Magics settled into the lower quarter of the town, it became a somewhat coveted location to live and visit. The town had its share of slums and alleys that I didn't travel down alone at night, but it was mostly nice and safe.

Before the population exploded, Hallow's Promise had one inn—the Siren's Sorrow. Its basic accommodations got the job done. The kitchen supplied ale and bread. The rooms had a bed and a lock. Women would even warm the sheets in exchange for some coins. But as the town grew, better inns stretched down Main Street. The Sorrow evolved from a central point for weary travelers to a hinge point for the underground and unsavory.

The wooden building looked out of place among the newer structures on Main Street. A carved siren sat in the front, holding a long-faded sign. I'd never really looked at her before, but the oil lanterns along the streets cast shadows beneath her tawny eyes.

I related to that. The shadows under my own eyes felt even darker.

Ilene pulled at the neckline of her borrowed cloak. "I

still don't understand why I must wear such uncomfortable clothing."

"Well, are you willing to take the armor off?" I'd repeated the same words so many times, they started to sound like a mantra.

She stiffened. "Of course not. A soldier does not remove their armor in the midst of the battlefield."

I bit my tongue to avoid telling her *again* that there was no battle in Hallow's Promise. "Do you want everyone to report to the marshal that there's a woman wearing armor with a rebel insignia walking around town?"

"That sounds likely to delay my quest."

"Yes, it would delay your quest quite significantly. Since you won't take off the armor, and you don't want to sit in a prison cell waiting for the king to decapitate you." She flinched at those words, finally showing some hint of self-preservation. "Then you have to wear the cloak to hide the armor."

Hide was a strong word. The stretched wool fabric barely covered the heavy metal, but it was enough to smother the etched insignias.

Ilene straightened. Her perfect lips parted for another jab at the cloak, but Krissa spoke first.

"I think you look good," she said. A blush turned golden in the oil lights, staining her cheeks immediately. "I mean . . . the cloak. I think the cloak looks good. Not that you don't also look good, I just wasn't trying to be so specific . . ." Krissa turned to me with her eyes wide in horror.

I avoided pressing the palm of my hand into my face. Barely.

But Ilene turned to the woman on my other side. Her gaze narrowed and her head tipped, like maybe she hadn't really *seen* Krissa earlier, even though Krissa's rainbow ensemble was difficult to miss. Twists of colors wrapped around her legs from the long skirt, which led to an equally unique sweater. Ribbons lined her hair, forming a halo around her head.

Ilene, the Phoenix Queen, stood a little straighter. A brilliant smile pushed her lips upward. I had half a mind to smother the lanterns on the street. They weren't nearly bright enough when compared to the glow illuminating from the woman's face.

"Thank you," she said, strong and confident.

Krissa's mouth fell open. She looked away from Ilene and sucked a ragged breath through clenched teeth.

I leaned my head back and studied the stars. Maybe one of them would fall to earth and crush me immediately.

Of course, I had no such luck.

"Let's go inside already."

The scent of spilled ale and smoke greeted us as I pulled the door open. People mingled through the wide space. Most settled around the spattering of tables, laughing and drinking over a round of cards or dice. Others talked near the flickering flames of the giant fireplace along the rear wall.

Nobody looked up as two regular sized women and one giant in barely concealed rebel armor walked inside. Just another day at the Siren's Sorrow.

"Come in, dears, and shut the door before the cold gets in," the woman at the bar spoke before looking up. A smile crossed Lillie's face when she noticed us, but her gaze caught on Ilene and her eyes widened.

I sighed. Time to accept this reaction, since it would probably occur everywhere Ilene went.

"Hi, Lillie." I leaned against the bar.

She ignored me completely. "Who's that?"

I tracked her gaze to . . . Ilene. Of course.

"A friend."

She blinked.

I pressed my lips together. Clearly, progressing in finding Valen was going to stall if Ilene distracted everyone.

I turned. "Hey." Ilene looked at me, all the intensity of her gaze weighing through the same blue eyes I'd grown rather fond of. "Why don't you two pick out a table while I talk?"

Krissa pointed at Ilene, then back to herself. "*Us?*"

"Yes." I stressed the word. Krissa's mouth gaped, but Ilene turned away without a word. My friend hesitated a moment longer, then trudged down the part Ilene created through the crowd.

Lillie's gaze refocused on me once the distraction left. She blinked, and her lips pursed.

"What kind of trouble have you gotten into now, dear?"

I shrugged. "I'm looking for Valen. Have you seen him lately?"

Valen ran with the underground circuit that frequented the Siren's Sorrow. He used the illicit activities of the town to gather and distribute information about the rebellion—a fact I'd very recently learned during our last case. Lillie, of course, knew everything that happened inside the Sorrow.

She tapped one finger against her chin. "Now that you mention it, it's been a while since Valen's shown up here."

"How about Adora Bolivar?"

Lillie's face flattened. "She's dead. You know that."

"Sure. Do you know anyone that can pass a message to the dead?"

"Doesn't everyone? But it's a bit early for Dy to show up here." She glanced out the window—which happened to be in the same direction where Krissa and Ilene sat together at a little table. Only darkness filtered through the glass panes. "You'll have to wait for him."

"Thank you, Lillie. We'll also take a round of ales and a loaf of bread." I set the coins on the counter as she nodded and shuffled toward the kitchen—with only a single glance back toward Ilene.

I sucked in a deep breath. The second floor of the Sorrow housed rooms for overnight stays. Valen and I had once shared a room during a murder investigation—not by my choice. Distant memories of his voice and his body beside me rose to the surface. My heart clenched. I had to find him, and he had to be alive or . . .

I didn't want to think about the consequences. The capital forbid my specific magic. The king sentenced anyone with necromantic magic to death immediately. But he had needed me to keep him alive. I'd spent years in the depths of Erline transferring life from prisoners into the king to buy him a few more heartbeats.

If I used my magic, the king would sense my location immediately. He'd send his elite guards—the Providers—to find me and haul me back.

My arm itched at the thought. I'd been one of the king's Providers before fleeing the capital. A few weeks ago, Valen had used his magic to turn the dagger tattoo on my forearm into a shimmering gold color, and it hadn't faded. My concealment spell kept the mark invisible, but I knew his golden light spread across my skin.

If Valen was dead, theoretically, I could bring him back to life. It would cost me everything I'd built in Hallow's Promise. The king would hunt and kill anyone that knew about my power.

"Here, love." Lillie set a loaf of bread in a metal tin on the counter. Thick wads of salty butter trailed across the top, making my mouth water. "I'll bring the ales to the table in a moment."

"Thanks." I scooped up the food and meandered through throngs of people toward Krissa and Ilene.

Krissa's hands were clamped together and perched beneath her chin. Her chocolate brown eyes widened into large disks while she hung on Ilene's every word.

"And then the man fell to his knees. Blood streamed from his mouth while he begged for mercy. But those that wear the king's insignia will never find mercy at my hand." She drew the longsword from her side and flicked the tip of the blade dramatically. "And I told him exactly that as my sword greeted his neck and detached it from his body."

Oh my.

Heads turned toward our table. Some patrons drew their own weapons and hid them discreetly with furrowed brows. I bet they sized Ilene up and didn't like their odds of survival.

I smiled and pushed Ilene's hand down, lowering the blade. "You're causing a scene," I whispered.

The woman blinked and glanced around. She had the decency to blush slightly and put the weapon away.

"My apologies." She ducked her head at me. "I'm used to recanting victories among the soldiers."

"I thought it was enthralling," Krissa said. She sounded a little out of breath.

I narrowed my eyes and studied her. Krissa didn't even turn when I sank into the open seat beside her. The firelight danced in her dark eyes as she stared at Ilene. A soft sigh escaped from her parted lips.

Hm. Something was up with her, and I'd figure it out as soon as we found Valen.

"Dy isn't here yet. We're going to wait for him."

Ilene reached for the bread first, and served a portion to Krissa, then me. She inhaled deeply and smiled. "This smells much better than the battlefield slop I've been eating."

"You mean you're not devouring the bodies of your enemies?"

She jerked her gaze to me and relaxed when I smiled. "I've found the years of corruption make the meat too tough."

Lillie brought the ales, and we ate, sipped, and laughed softly. A quiet comradery spread around the table. The common goal of finding Valen brought us together, but the realization that we had the same values, morals, and dark sense of humor made it all feel easy. I wished the mercenary was here to introduce me to his sister himself. A Valen-shaped hole tugged at my heart.

We would find him. We had to.

The door opened, and Krissa's spine straightened. I followed her stare over my shoulder.

Dymetri lingered in the doorway. His gaze swept over our table, ignoring the other questionable patrons drinking and gambling in the room. He wore all black with a short sword on his hip, looking as dangerous and deadly as he did last time we'd met.

But a new expression twisted his face: fear.

My brow creased as I stood and stepped toward the man. He tracked my approach briefly, but his gaze darted back to our table.

To Ilene.

Dy turned around and sprinted out of the doorway.

I froze as my mind tried to comprehend the scene. The

hardened criminal looked scared of the woman in the black cloak.

A blur of darkness ran past me. Ilene pulled open the front door and sprinted into the night.

I blinked. What just happened?

"Rae!" Krissa grabbed my arm. "We have to follow them!"

"Damn it!" I wrapped her hand in mine, and we ran, too.

Chapter 4

Dy and Ilene ran through the darkened streets with only oil lanterns lighting their shapes. They were both faster than me, which made sense as a hardened criminal and rebellion leader probably ran more than a potion maker turned Crime Investigation Expert.

They turned a corner, and I lost them for a moment. I cursed the black cloak I'd forced Ilene to wear. The shiny armor would have been easier to see than the thick wool. Next time, I'd pick a red or yellow cloak.

My lungs heaved and sharp stabs of pain pierced my side as I caught up to the sprinting pair. I fared better than Krissa, who fell behind immediately.

Dy dashed around another bend. Ilene lunged forward, both feet peeling away from the ground.

Time slowed. I forgot about breathing and pain as the woman flew over the cobblestone road with both arms outstretched. Her face twisted into a hard expression of determination. Dy's legs moved too slow. His gaze locked forward. I stammered to a stop, too busy watching to remember to run.

Dy's lips rounded as Ilene grabbed his shoulders. He twisted for a look—disbelief creasing his brows—and the pair fell to the ground together.

I blinked. I couldn't help it—it was impressive. Ilene had jumped high enough to lock both arms around the taller man's shoulders and effortlessly force him into the ground. She did it all while wearing slabs of heavy armor. Not even a touch of magic aided her.

Krissa stopped beside me. Her chest heaved.

"Wow. She's incredible."

I nodded. There was no other explanation.

Ilene rolled Dymetri onto his back. The man whimpered from his grounded position, and the sound snapped me out of the stupor Ilene's mobility had lulled me into. I hurried to the pair and crouched beside Dy's head.

"Hey, Dy. How's it going?"

His wild gaze snapped to me. Emotions flashed across his face, too fast for me to follow. Finally, he parted his lips. "Do you *know* who this is?"

"Yes."

My reply fell to deaf ears.

"This is Ilene—"

I clamped my hand over his mouth and glanced over my shoulder. Our pursuit had trailed into the street behind the Siren's Sorrow onto the edge of the Shrine District. Little houses in neat rows surrounded us. It was far from a private place and shouting Ilene's identity into the street wouldn't help us avoid the Sheriff's attention.

"Shut up or you'll get us all killed." His mouth moved beneath my hand, releasing muffled noises. "Will you be quiet if I let you talk?"

He nodded, and I moved my hand.

Dy lowered his voice. "If you know who she is, then you know we're all condemned to death."

"A little dramatic, Dy, don't you think?" He flinched at the sound of his own nickname, as though the word felt too close to his current fears. "Listen, we just need a favor."

"This is a funny way to ask for one, Rae, by bringing death straight to my doorstep."

I touched Ilene's arm. "You can let him up."

Her eyes narrowed. "He may run again."

"Then you can chase him and tackle him again. I have a feeling he wouldn't get very far."

Ilene gave one stern nod. "That's right." She stood in an easy motion.

Dy sucked in a breath, and I held my hand out. The man studied me for a heartbeat, then grabbed my palm and I helped him stand.

Last time I'd seen Dy, he'd been cocky, arrogant, and dangerous. Tonight, he didn't look like any of those things. His black tunic was disheveled from more than Ilene's less-than-gentle handling. The curling locks of his hair were greasy and tangled.

"Tell me what you want so I can get out of here." Stress layered his words, his usual smooth voice tight and hard. I'd make a high wager that something other than Ilene's appearance had shaken the man.

"I need to know if you've seen Valen recently."

He snorted. "No, Rae, I haven't seen the Nightwrath in over a fortnight, and neither has anyone else."

My heart sank, and a rock lodged in my throat. I fought to keep my voice steady. "Why not?"

"Because he's missing, just like the rest of them."

Darkness wrapped around the edges of my vision. Not even the keeper of secrets in Hallow's Promise knew where Valen was.

Krissa stepped beside me, but I barely felt the movement against my arm. "What do you mean, the rest of them?"

Dy stepped closer to us, releasing a hint of an orange and honey scent beneath layers of salty sweat. "Nobody will admit anything, but those of us in the shadows are disappearing. One after another. Not only those that work for her—" He jerked a finger toward Ilene, who crossed her arms. "But anyone that barters in things other than coins."

"I . . . I haven't heard anything about people going missing." Besides Valen.

He snorted and straightened out his tunic. A bit of the old Dy peered through his eyes and we winked at me. "You wouldn't, would you? Nobody notices when one shadow consumes another. Nobody cares."

People were going missing in Hallow's Promise, and nobody noticed because they were outside of the law.

My heart softened. Most people found themselves in such a place because of circumstances beyond their control. Everyone deserved to be seen.

"I care." I reached toward Dy's arm, but he stepped back. "I care about you and about them." And about Valen. "I'm going to look into this."

He gave me a killer smile—one that would have made other women melt in their boots from either temptation or fear. "You're welcome to look at me whenever and wherever you want, Rae. But leave this alone. The Nightwrath is gone and accepting that will keep you alive."

"I can't. I have to find him."

"Why? He's nobody to you. He's a spy, a mercenary. He has more kills than he'll ever have lovers. You're better off without him."

I smiled, because Dymetri had it all wrong. Valen was a spy—for the rebellion against a corrupt king and the government that tore apart families to protect its own power. He was a mercenary—using his honed skills and deadly power to kill even more dangerous people and crawl into the underground places to gather information against Erline.

Valen had given me my sword because he believed in my abilities to help others. When Tyfin couldn't train me anymore, Valen stepped up and sharpened my skills with the blade. He challenged me, tempted me, and drove me crazy.

And I didn't care how many kills or lovers he'd had. I needed to find him.

Smoke oozed from the sword at my side. I hid my shock as it enveloped me in dark shadows. It had smoked before, but only during a fight. Misty tendrils peeled from the metal and escaped through the leather sheath to wrap around my legs, my arms, my neck.

"I will hear no more of this." I let common magic seep into my voice and harden it, keeping it low enough that eavesdroppers inside nearby houses wouldn't hear more than murmuring. "I will find the Nightwrath, and you will help me."

His knees trembled. "What do you want from me?"

The smoke solidified and wrapped around us. It flickered and flashed until it matched the lantern-lit night perfectly, blocking us from the view of any wandering eyes.

"You will tell Adora Bolivar that I am searching for her."

Dy blinked. "That's all you want me to do?"

"Uh . . . yes."

He rolled his eyes and gestured at me. "The smoke, the voice, all because you want me to pass Adora a message? All you had to do was ask."

The smoke faded, as did my enthusiasm in the conversation. "You were being difficult." The words sounded defensive, even to me.

"Yeah, you three chased me, tackled me, and smoked at me. That would scare anyone shitless! Next time, try asking me, Rae." He winked at Krissa as he turned away from us. "I'm happy to accommodate *anything,* if you just ask. Dy doesn't say no to pretty women. I'll give Adora your message." He pointed at Ilene. "Just don't bring her here again."

"Deal," I said, but Dy was already walking away.

Chapter 5

Ilene turned to me. "What was the smoke?"

"I don't know." I pulled my sword out of the sheath, but the smoke had stopped oozing. "It does that sometimes."

"May I?" She held her hand out.

I placed the hilt into her hand, but its absence felt wrong, like an itch that couldn't be scratched. Her fingers curled around the wrapping.

She hissed and let it go.

I blinked. "What was that?"

"It doesn't like me." She rubbed her palm along the rough fabric of the cloak.

"What does that mean? It's a sword."

Ilene gestured to Krissa. "See if it likes her more."

I shrugged and held the sword out to my friend. She eyed it. "I've never held a sword."

"You just grab it here—but be careful. It's heavier than it looks."

Krissa still didn't move. Ilene reached over and gripped her hand, carefully cradling my friend's palm. "You let the bindings on the hilt rest in the center of the hand. Pull the grip closer to the bottom, where the guards are. Perfect. Now, hold it just like this." Ilene used her hand to close Krissa's fingers around the hilt.

"Thanks," Krissa murmured, her voice breathy. I creased my brows and studied her face. Even the glowing lanterns couldn't hide the pinkness staining her cheeks.

Krissa's eyes widened. "Oh!"

I tensed, searching for an injury. Maybe she's slipped over the guards and cut herself . . . But her skin was flawless, her grip firm and in the correct place.

"Oh!" This time she giggled. "It likes me!"

"You're both crazy," I said. "It's a *sword*. It doesn't like or dislike anyone."

Ilene gently took the blade from Krissa and handed it back to me with a grimace. "Yes, it's just a regular sword, the same way you're a regular witch. Is that correct?"

I pulled the weapon back. It felt warm in my hand. "You don't know me."

"I know you are no ordinary witch. I know the sentient objects were hunted and burned long ago, yet a quaint little wagon I visited this morning certainly had a mind of its own."

Brew. She'd recognized whatever spark of my magic that made Brew what it was.

My heart thumped in my chest. This woman was becoming more dangerous to my livelihood than only being the leader of a rebellion. If she knew the truth about me, she held everything I loved in her hand.

"Stop talking about things you do not understand," I said.

Ilene grabbed my arm. Her grip was firm, not hard. "My brother spent a period of time in Erline. He spoke of its cruelty, but also of an unexpected beauty. Your magic feels similar to that. Life, death, it's only power. The beauty is how you use it. You've been using your magic to build yourself a family."

I pulled away from her. The secrets she spoke so blatantly had been carefully guarded for the years I'd lived in Hallow's Promise. I wasn't ready to sacrifice my safety or my friends' safety because she thought she knew better than I did.

"I can't use my magic." I pulled up my sleeve, dropping the concealment spell. The dagger tattoo marking me as a Provider of the king glowed gold on my arm. I held it up to her face. "Using any of my own magic will bring the king straight here. We'd never find Valen, your rebellion would fail, and we'd all die. Do you understand any of that, Ilene? Or does the Phoenix Queen only rise from the ashes of the people she gets killed?"

Her gaze softened. I clenched my fists. I didn't want her pity.

"Your magic is not something you can avoid. It leaks from you, Rae, into the very parts of your life. The wagon has a sentience. The sword does now, too."

I had too much anger for the words to impact me. Later, when it was quiet enough to think, I would decipher the meaning of what she said.

Now, I hated her. I hated that she said these dangerous things, that her presence here meant Valen was missing, that she looked so damn *calm* and *collected*.

"I'll find your brother." I clenched my teeth until they hurt. "But I'll do it alone. I never want to see you again."

I turned, aiming for the darkness, heading to nowhere.

Krissa touched my arm, but I shrugged her off. I didn't want to be comforted. I wanted to burn from the inside out. I wanted to scream and run and deny everything Ilene said.

I escaped into the night, and the billowing smoke from the sword in my hand followed me all the way home.

* * *

I had a magic sword.

I sighed and hit my forehead against Brew's countertop again and again. Maybe hitting it enough times would wake me up from the nightmare currently unfolding.

The countertop billowed beneath my head and softened. Brew vibrated unhappily beneath me. It didn't like that I tried to hurt myself.

I sighed again. I had a magic sword and a magic wagon.

"Um, excuse me. The sign says that you're open, but you seem to be . . . busy?" A customer stood on her tiptoes and peeked into the gaping sash at the side of the wagon.

"Sorry." I dragged myself upright. "It was a long night. What can I get you?"

"Ugh, I get that. It's exam week and I don't think I slept at all last night. Why does the History of Toxic Herbs and Botanicals require an essay exam? Ludicrous, if you ask me. Which, of course, no one does. Anyway, I'll have the Feeling MUG-gy."

The smile across my lips was fake. "Absolutely, it'll be just a moment."

I'd moped all night about what Ilene had said. When I got up, Bubbles hopped to the door like it was any other day, and I followed him out to Brew. Making tea was more productive than sitting at home, staring at my sword.

Instead, I stood inside Brew and stared at my sword.

The metal didn't move as I reached for the cauldron of water bubbling on the inset fire. No smoke oozed out while I ruffled through the upper cabinet and gathered all the herbs for the drink.

I pulled a container out of the magically chilled cupboard and rounded on the sword, like turning quickly enough would catch it in some kind of sentient action.

Nothing.

I set the jar on the counter and found a spoon. Thick balls filled the jar, wrapped in little layers of sticky sugar. I'd ordered them from a merchant that traveled between countries and brought the delicacy from far away. I tried to make my own, but the balls disintegrated the moment I added any sort of liquid, so I kept the merchant in business by buying all his stock.

Finding Valen wasn't going well. So far, I'd made an enemy of his sister, probably hurt Krissa's feelings, and discovered that his disappearance went far deeper than I'd expected.

I filtered the black tea leaves into a little mesh bag and hung it over the edge of a mug. Water sloshed around the cauldron as I lifted it and poured in enough liquid to submerge the herbs. The water darkened immediately.

Talking to Leof was the next logical step in my investigation—until Adora responded to my message. The marshal would know about other missing person reports. I didn't want to get the law or my werewolf friend involved, though. Leof cared about me—in more ways than just friendship. He'd want to handle the investigation himself, to avoid putting me in danger.

I swirled a heavy amount of thick cream into the tea, which I'd scraped from the top of fresh milk this morning. The drink softened from black to light tan. I added the little balls, which sank to the bottom of the cup. Chips of ice followed on top, and I planted a neat flower into the cubes.

Making tea was simple. Every other part of life was hard.

"Here you go." I forced the smile back on. The customer

didn't seem to notice that it looked more like a scowl.

"Thank you! Say, I don't think I've seen this wagon here before, and trust me, I'd remember such a cute little shop like this. Have you moved here recently? Do you plan to stay here for a while? I'd love to come back tomorrow. Also, is your sword smoking?"

I cut my gaze to the weapon, which was indeed billowing gray tendrils across the counter. I pulled it below the countertop and out of sight, making my smile brighter.

"Looks like the towel behind the sword caught a little fire, sorry about that, I've put it out now." She looked doubtful, so I launched into the rest of her questions to distract from the truth. "I used to sell my drinks on the main campus, but the dean and I had a . . . disagreement. Now I've been selling on this side of the road and it's going really well. A lot of customers come through the gate every morning. Did you mention your name? I'm afraid it slipped my mind."

Her smile didn't miss a beat. "I didn't mention it, actually, but you can call me Elo, everyone does."

"Nice to meet you, Elo. What are you studying?"

The Central Campus for Mages and Magics sprawled across the lower corner of Hallow's Promise. It offered beautiful, sculpted lawns, a coveted education in the magical arts, and armfuls of students hungry for any liquid promising to help them survive the semester. I used to sell on the campus—until I'd angered the dean . . . through hardly any fault of my own.

Her eyes flashed. "I haven't totally decided yet. Maybe I'll try out potions." She glanced at the parts of Brew visible through the sash.

She didn't mention anything more about the sword, which hopefully meant my distraction worked.

"Good luck with your exams," I said. Elo nodded and passed along her coins, apparently accepting the words as the farewell I intended. When she turned around the corner, I pulled the sash down. A click echoed through the wagon as Brew pushed the lock into place.

"Thanks." I patted the countertop. I didn't feel like making tea anymore. Pretending everything was normal when it felt like my life was on the verge of ripping apart wasn't working.

I sank to the wooden floor, which put me eye to eye with Bubbles.

The warplog yawned as a greeting, and I stroked a soft touch across his smooth skin. His red tongue dashed out to lick both eyeballs while maintaining strict eye contact—basically the way Bubbles said *I love you.*

"Should we get you something to eat?"

His eyes illuminated in excitement. I wasn't sure the warplog understood anything I said, but maybe he recognized the tone of my voice when I suggested food.

First, I would feed the warplog. Then, I'd talk to Leof at the Station about the missing criminals. Last, I'd find Krissa and apologize.

So, what if I had a magic wagon and a magic sword. I also had a warplog and a best friend, and I'd die before I lost any of them.

Chapter 6

Bubbles hopped along behind me, drawn forward by the scent of putrid meat in my hand. Matilda had wrapped the giant leg bone in paper, but the sickly-sweet stench of decay still trailed behind me.

It was Bubbles' favorite smell.

Our progress from the butcher's shop in the center of Main Street toward the Sheriff's Station perched at its very edge was slow because Bubbles kept stopping and trying to open his gaping mouth every few steps. When he realized that I—and, therefore, the meat he wanted to devour—kept moving, he'd snap his jaw shut and manage a few more hops.

Acid drool pooled in dollops behind us when we finally reached the Station. I passed Castor in the hall before Leof's office, and the constable glared at me.

"Rae," he said as we passed. "Your company is less pleasant every time I see you."

"Castor." I gave him my sweetest smile and hesitated at his side. He leaned away with a grimace, but refused to budge away from me. "You should watch out. My warplog is hungry, and he eats anything that *stinks*."

The man grunted. "Then maybe you're the one that should—"

His words cut off mid-insult. "What the hell is that?"

Ah, I'd stopped too long, and Bubbles interpreted the pause as mealtime. His greenish skin peeled away from his lipless mouth and exposed rows of ragged, razor teeth. Chunks of bone clung to some of the sharpened tips from his previous meal. The harsh stench of acid made the air smell like the color green. His mouth stretched impossibly wide compared to the size of his body.

"Don't worry, I'd never feed him anything as vile as you." I tossed the leg chunk into the black hole of Bubbles' mouth, paper and all. "You'd give the poor guy heartburn."

The warplog shut his mouth with a snap and a sleepy expression crossed his face. He always napped after a big meal, so I scooped him into my arms.

Castor skirted along the wall, away from us. "Leof, your pet freak is here!" he shouted down the hall before disappearing into an adjacent door.

Bubbles opened one eye and stared at where the man had just been. I tapped the rounded space where a slight protrusion marked the creature's nose.

"Someday you'll get to eat him, but not today."

His eyes feathered closed at the promise, and his little chest rose and fell against my palm.

I opened the door to Leof's office without knocking. Heat immediately soaked through my clothing from the giant fireplace on the opposite wall. Some of my anxiety soothed away just by stepping inside. I'd worked through many cases in this room, perched in one of the leather chairs before the fire, with Leof chatting softly at my side.

The wolf didn't look up as I closed the door. Usually, I found him at the sturdy desk to the side of the room, but today, he sat in the other chair and watched the flames.

I took my usual seat. Leof smiled. The werewolf's face was probably softer at some point, but the years of investigating murder and trauma turned his expression hard. Little lines gathered at the edges of his eyes, but they may have been created by his young daughter rather than the job.

Bubbles flopped onto my lap and turned over to present his tummy for some scratches. I trailed my fingers lightly over his skin, and he sighed.

"I ran into Castor in the hall."

"I'm sorry." Leof chuckled. "Is he still alive?"

"For now. Where's Suzie?"

The marshal shrugged. "Who knows. If she's not with you, she's usually at one of her friends' places."

Suzie was Leof's daughter and my very unofficial apprentice. She wanted to know more about her magic, self-defense, and the finer parts of death. I happened to be the only available teacher.

The silence that settled between us was comfortable. Leof had saved me when I'd fled Erline and wandered into Hallow's Promise. First, he'd given me a job and a legitimate way to earn money. Then, he'd let buy my land and house from him. He'd seen me when nobody else did, and he'd walked me to the library to return the plethora of books I'd stolen. Leof had never judged me for what I'd needed to do at that time of my life.

I loved the man, undoubtedly. We were friends, for sure, but a few things had happened recently that made me wonder if we could be more than friends.

"Valen is missing." I broke the silence.

"I'm not surprised." In fact, he sounded a little gleeful.

"Maybe he's finally moved on."

Valen wouldn't leave me—not of his own free will.

"I talked to Dymetri at the Siren's Sorrow last night."

"I wish you wouldn't go to that place. Didn't a shape-shifting murderer attack you last time you went there?" His fist clenched as though wishing to cradle a strong glass of booze.

"Not the last time, it was the time before that."

His face turned red.

I continued. "Dymetri says Valen isn't the only one that's gone missing."

"The only what?"

I shrugged. "Criminal, mercenary, someone who won't be missed. I figured you'd know if reports were being filed."

Leof surged from his seat. I tensed as his amber eyes caught mine. Leof had iron-tight control over the wolf he shared his soul with, but strong emotions brought the animal to the surface.

"Damn it, Rae. You can't get involved with that."

I froze. Bubbles shifted, sensing the change in my demeanor in his sleep.

"It's true? People are going missing?"

Leof banged his fist on the corner of his desk. "Not ordinary people, Rae. The worst of the worst are disappearing from Hallow's Promise. At first, we thought it was just good luck. But there's too many for it to be anything less than a pattern."

A mix of anger and frustration bubbled in my gut. It took my entire willpower, and Bubbles' cute sleeping face, to keep me seated.

"You *knew* people were being taken, and you didn't tell me anything?"

"This is not something you want to be involved with. Castor

and I have been looking into it. The Sheriff is even here from the capital to manage the investigation personally. These are dangerous people, Rae, and whatever is happening to them is even worse."

I shook my head. "You can't keep me in the dark, Leof. It's my job to investigate crime in this city, regardless of how unsavory the victims might be."

"Unsavory." He laughed at the word. "This isn't like biting into a bad apple. These *victims* have killed innocents for looking at them the wrong way. I can't let you get hurt."

The anger turned to tremors down my legs and I had to stand. Bubbles shifted from my arms to the chair and curled away from me, straight back to sleep.

"You don't get to decide what I do, Leof. This is *Valen*. He's missing, maybe hurt . . ." Or worse, but I refused to say that. "I'm going to do whatever it takes to find him."

Leof ran a hand across his face. When he lowered it, the man looked older, more tired, almost defeated. "Please, don't. I can't take care of you around danger like that."

Suddenly, I envied children and their ability to acceptably scream in public. "I can take care of myself. I have a magic sword now."

He blinked. "What?"

I'd never told Leof plainly about my necromancy. But the marshal was a smart man. He'd seen the incredible things Brew was capable of and had probably figured out my true abilities long ago. And he still wanted to be my friend, even if that meant potential death if the king found me.

"Ile—someone told me that since I'm not using my magic, it's just pouring out of me on its own. Apparently, whatever happened to Brew is happening to the sword, too."

"I don't even know what to say to that," Leof finally answered. "The king can't sense this excess magic?"

"He's not here, is he?" I held my arms out. "Tell me everything you know about the disappearances."

"There's not much to know." Leof gave into his temptation and produced a flask from somewhere inside his desk. A glass followed, and he poured a healthy amount of golden liquid. He signed with the first sip. "Most of our information is from rumors, and informants suddenly going missing. It was a while before I realized something was wrong."

I took the leather chair Leof had vacated. I didn't want to risk waking up Bubs. "Did you go to any of the scenes?"

"Of course. Nothing, not a hint of magic or anything. It's like they vanished into thin air."

"Witnesses?"

Leof shook his head.

"Interviews?"

He shrugged. "These aren't the friendliest people toward the Sheriff's Station, Rae. More than a couple spat on me rather than answering my questions."

"Where's the most recent scene?"

His eyes softened, and he took another sip. Maybe it was more of a gulp. "I'm asking again, please, do not get involved in this."

"Where was it, Leof? If I have to ask around to find it, that's even more potential danger."

He flinched. I wanted to feel bad, but I was still mad he'd kept this case a secret.

"It was at Pledge Lane, near the gate. There's nothing there, though. I already checked."

I nodded. Leof was a good investigator and would have been

thorough. But I had a different set of skills entirely.

"Thanks, Leof. If it makes you feel better, I won't start my investigation until tomorrow."

"That doesn't really help, but why wait?"

"I need to make some apologies tonight. I was mean to Krissa . . ." And Ilene, but mentioning the rebellion leader would put Leof in an awkward position. "Can you keep an eye on Bubbles?"

We both looked at the sleeping warplog. His rear foot twitched.

"Sure." Leof's voice was tight with resignation. I knew he wanted to say more, but short of putting me in one of the cells beneath the Station—which a certain Nightengale actually destroyed—he couldn't stop me.

"He's going to regurgitate some bones in a few hours. I'd recommend putting him outside or else he'll chew them to shards all over your office."

I fled and slammed the door, but Leof's cursing still slipped through.

Chapter 7

Krissa lived on the edge of Consecrate Quarter, which hugged the west side of the Central Campus of Mages and Magics. It gave her an easy walk to her job as a professor on the campus, but made the trek from the Sheriff's Station a bit longer.

I appreciated the journey tonight. Spring was slowly winning the battle against the winter cold. Tiny buds sprouted along the barren trees. Snow clung to the shadows, melting slightly where the afternoon sun kissed the perimeter. The sun sank toward Spirit's Peak—the only mountain within Hallow's Promise's city wall. The air smelled like fresh water and the promise of rain.

Guilt chewed on me from the inside. Ilene's presence threatened my friends and my life here, but I'd been mean to Krissa. I remembered the feel of her hand as I shrugged away from her. I abandoned her with Ilene, a stranger, and had simmered in my own anger rather than taking care of my friend.

It hurt. I thought I'd changed in the last year.

Apparently not.

I mulled over apologies as I walked. I wanted to say something short and meaningful. Maybe I'd end by begging for forgiveness. It didn't matter that the anger came from fear.

I feared for Krissa's life, and that it would end because of her friendship with me.

A soft crunch of a breaking stick was my only warning before I slammed into someone else on the road.

I staggered back, mindless apologies on the tip of my tongue. The other person released a surprised squeal—one I recognized instantly.

"Krissa!"

"Rae!"

She swayed on her feet, and I grabbed her arm to steady her. "What are you doing here?"

"I was going to see you, of course." Rainbow ribbons curled around her face with the warm breeze, and she brushed them away. "What are you doing?"

My heart clenched. There were a million reasons she'd look for me, and few of them were good.

"I was . . . looking for you."

Silence spanned between us. I still held her arm, and she didn't pull away. I should have let go, but my fingers refused to uncurl.

"Krissa, I'm so sorry." All the carefully scripted apologies I'd rehearsed on the way here liquified and spilled out of my mind. "I'm sorry that I was angry, and that I was mean to you yesterday. I'm sorry that I abandoned you with Ilene. That I'm putting you in danger by being your friend. I understand if you want to yell at me, or say you never want to see me again. Please, if you tell me to leave, I'll never bother you again."

Her brown eyes widened, and a little tug pulled one side of her lips up. She shifted, grabbing my hand in both of hers.

"Rae, I was coming to apologize to *you*."

My heart skipped a beat. "Why? *You* didn't do anything

wrong."

"Yes, I did." She squeezed my fingers. "Ilene angered you, and I just stood there and watched. I know how you feel about your past. It was wrong of me to let her upset you, then watch you walk away alone. I'm here for you. You're my best friend. I'm not going to allow that to happen again."

Hot tears filled my eyes. I wanted to brush them away, but Krissa had captured my other hand too, so they spilled over my eyelids and trailed down my cheeks. She searched my face, studying the little rivers, and pulled me into a hug.

I clung to her. "I don't deserve you," I whispered into her chestnut hair and rainbow ribbons.

"I wouldn't let you be best friends with anyone else." She pulled me tighter. "We're both human, Rae. We're going to screw up, over and over again. It doesn't mean we're not worth loving."

At the capital, making a mistake meant punishment, torture, death. Love hadn't been in my vocabulary during the formative years of my life. Sometimes, it was hard to remember even now.

A little creature brushed against my ankle. I blinked through the tears enough to see Whiskers rubbing his quills along my leg. It was as comforting a gesture as a Nightingale could manage.

Krissa pulled away but kept my hand in hers. "Where's Bubbles?"

"He just ate and wouldn't want to hop this far."

"You didn't take Brew?"

I wiped the tears and shook my head. "I wanted to walk. It gave me time to think. Where's Ilene? Where did she end up staying?"

A little blush filled Krissa's face. "She stayed at my place. On the couch," she added, though I hadn't asked. "I went this way because I figured you'd talked to Leof about Valen's case. If you weren't at the Sheriff's Station, I planned to check Brew's usual spots. You wouldn't have escaped me, even if you'd wanted to."

"I hadn't wanted to. I never will."

"Good. What did you learn from Leof?"

I snorted and the last of the tears evaporated in the weakening sunshine. "He told me that it's too dangerous to search for Valen and I should let it go."

"Does he know you at all?"

"Apparently not. I left Bubbles there so he can throw up bone shards all over the office floor."

"Good, he deserves that."

"He did tell me where one of the disappearances occurred." I tugged Krissa forward, and she followed, unquestioning. "Do you want to go check it out?"

"Search a crime scene where one dangerous criminal mysteriously kidnapped—or possibly killed—another?" Her lips curled into a brilliant smile. "Absolutely, I do."

* * *

Two main roads ran east and west through Hallow's Promise. Pledge Lane was near the aptly named North Gate. It also passed along the perimeter of The Void and dead-ended before hitting the dirt road to my house in the East Brim.

"Where exactly did Leof say this abduction happened?" Krissa kicked a chunk of ice to the side of the road.

"He didn't."

"Uh, huh. And did he mention witnesses?"

". . . no."

"Of course. How about who, exactly, was taken?"

I sighed. "Also, no."

"So, we don't know what to look for, where to look, or who we're looking for?"

I pressed a finger into my temple, where a splitting headache was starting to develop. "He said it was by the gate."

"We've wandered past the gate five times. Maybe we should ask the gate guards? They were incredibly helpful last time."

Last time I asked the guards for help, they mocked us, and I considered killing one of them. Since then, my control had grown impeccably, probably.

My friend stopped in the middle of the cobblestone road and studied me. "You got flustered, didn't you?"

"I did not get *flustered*." My cheeks turned hot. "I was the epitome of calm and collected."

Krissa tapped her finger against her chin. "No, you got flustered, I know it. You can't talk to Leof about Valen. It's a conflict of interests. And whatever Leof said made you flustered."

"Would you stop saying that word? Illegal necromancers get annoyed or agitated. We do *not* get flustered."

A smooth rock protruded from the mud and snow near the side of the road. Krissa hiked her skirt up, sending a cascade of rainbow colors around her feet, and perched on top. She turned wide eyes and pouting lips to me. "Tell me what the mean werewolf said."

No amount of prayers to any god would save me from Krissa's questions.

I sucked in a breath through my teeth. "He said that he can't keep me safe if I go looking for Valen."

"And how does that make you feel?"

I glared at her. "Bad."

She flicked her fingers. "I need more than that."

Truthfully, it made me feel confused. Leof trying to keep me safe should be a gift sprouted from our friendship. He was loyal and kind and generous.

But I'd had safety for the last five years since I'd run from the capital. Safety had only given me secrets, loneliness, and a general distrust of everyone around me. Valen's arrival stripped away the walls I'd built and hidden behind. He gave me a sword. He taught me how to use it.

I didn't need Leof to keep me safe. I could do it myself.

"Dedicated," I said out loud.

Her brows rose. "Okay, I hadn't expected that one. Dedicated how? Are you finally going to date Leof?"

"*No*. I'm dedicated to finding Valen. I know he's not dead. And maybe dedicated to . . . something else afterward."

"Something else, like what?"

Like maybe do something braver than I'd ever considered before.

I opened my mouth. "I—"

Krissa screamed. She sprung from her rock with a speed I'd never deemed possible.

"Ghost!"

I swiveled on my feet, eyes searching the shadows where she pointed. The weight of my sword stumbled into my hand before I had decided to unsheathe it.

Warmth spread from the wrapped hilt into my fingers. It felt good to brace the hard metal against my palm. My mind spun through the most beneficial stances and strikes for this situation. But how the hell do you fight a ghost?

The shadows shifted slightly between the trees in the direction we both watched. A hazy silhouette of a person solidified, revealing that it was most certainly not a ghost.

My heart thumped. For a moment, I imagined Valen would step from the tree line with his crooked smile and arrogant eyes. That he'd apologize for abandoning me for over two weeks. Maybe he'd run his fingertips along my cheek and our blend of hot and icy magic would intermix around us.

But as the soft sunlight illuminated the figure, I realized their stature was too short. They didn't set their hips just right to account for the heavy sword Valen carried. There wasn't nearly enough swagger in their step.

It wasn't Valen escaping from the shadows.

I thought my heart couldn't hurt any more.

"I hear you're looking for me," the feminine voice said. She reached up to the dark hood and pushed it down.

Adora Bolivar cocked one hand on her hip and smiled brightly at us.

Chapter 8

Last time I'd unexpectedly met Adora, she'd shoved a dagger into my back and tried to lead me into the depths of the woods. Sure, I'd gotten the upper hand eventually, but this meeting was a great improvement.

Krissa, Whiskers, Ilene, Bubbles, Adora, and I all trekked through ragged forest paths in the confines of night. An icy chill sent goosebumps across my skin. Somewhere, an owl cried a melancholy song over the quiet terrain. Each step led us deeper into Reverence Square.

Despite my new comfort with bladed weapons, Reverence Square housed a lot of places I'd rather never visit. It was where the poorest of Hallow's Promise ended up when they couldn't—or refused to—find help. The putrid conditions and absolute lack of hope festered the perfect breeding ground for black market trades, hallucinogenic substance cultivation, and general ruckus.

The perfect place for a mercenary's lair.

"When I stayed with Valen, he had some really wicked wards up." Adora picked her steps carefully, barely releasing the slightest crunch of a broken stick. Ilene and I held our own, but Krissa could pass for a frolicking ratcoo—a cross between a weasel and a very small elephant. Large feet, sharp teeth, and more of a thunderous stroll than a graceful glide.

"Would you be able to break 'really wicked wards,' Rae?" Krissa whispered. It was humorous—how her stomps were louder than the soft question.

I shrugged, even though the darkness concealed the motion. "I'll try. Having Ilene here might help, since her blood will be similar to Valen's."

Ilene had been oddly quiet since we'd departed Krissa's house a few hours after Adora found us on the road. I wondered if the ticking clock in my head matched one in her's. One that said Valen's chances of survival were already slim, and every minute we wandered through the forest ate away at a positive outcome.

Thinking about Valen's possible death made my heart lurch. I carefully wrapped up the thoughts and stored them in the back of my mind, where they couldn't distract me.

"We're here."

The tree line spit us onto a dirt road. Modest homes huddled along the pathway. Many shared walls with their neighbors, some barely had walls at all. Moonlight hid the neglected exteriors and untamed properties, but it did little to smother the scent of decay and desperation.

Nobody moved through the darkness besides us. Few people dared to venture through Reverence Square after sunset. Those that did often had nefarious agendas.

Sort of like us.

"Valen's place is at the end of this block." Adora led us further down the dirt road. The buildings fell into more disarray the further we trekked. Glowing lanterns and candles faded out until only shadows surrounded us. An itch crawled along my skin. Someone, or *something*, was watching us.

"Nice neighborhood your beau lives in." Krissa shoved her elbow into my side.

I rubbed the accosted spot. "He's not my beau."

"Yeah, it's perfectly normal to drop everything in your life, flock through the worst part of town, and consider running through wards that might peel your skin off for a man that you don't care about."

"I care about Valen." That was easy enough to admit.

Krissa snorted. "Whatever you say."

"Peel your skin off?" They were the first words Ilene had said tonight.

"It wouldn't surprise me." Krissa shrugged. "Your brother has a reputation for being intense."

But Ilene shook her head. "Valen designed his previous wards to boil the intruder's guts from the inside without killing them, so he had time to interrogate them. I find that the skin peeling would be rather tame for my brother."

Krissa gulped audibly.

"We're here," Adora announced, followed by a sigh. "But it looks like he still has the wards up. Which I guess is good. It means he's not dead."

'Here' was a quaint little house inset from the road. A tidy pathway strolled across the unkempt yard—minimal but functional. Darkness stained the foggy windows. No one was home.

"There's nothing here," Krissa said.

My brows creased as I studied my friend, then turned back to Valen's house.

Adora sighed. "Yeah, that's how I know the wards are up. If we try to cross onto the property with the intention of entering Valen's house, whatever spell he's etched into the wards will activate. And I certainly don't want my guts boiled."

"What are you talking about?" I gestured toward the house. "It's clearly right here."

Three sets of eyes locked on me. Actually, four, since Bubbles took the opportunity to stare at me and run his long tongue over one beady eyeball.

"You can see it?" Adora spoke slowly.

"Yes, of course. It's white with a brown door and a dirt path leading up the front." Everyone stared blankly at me. I sucked in a breath. "None of you can see the house?"

They all shook their heads.

"Oh." That was a neat ward. *When*—not if—we got Valen back, I'd make him teach me that one.

"He must have modified the ward to let you have access, Rae. He never did that when I stayed here. I could only enter the property when Valen was with me. Did he ever ask for a sample of your blood?"

"No, but he brought me here after a Shadow-Beast attacked me." I involuntarily glanced at the hoglet beneath my feet. The Nightingale was capable of ripping into other dimensions. A very bad woman used him to summon otherworldly beasts that attacked me. Valen saved my life. "I probably bled a lot then."

"You don't know for sure?"

"I wasn't exactly conscious. And I was drugged on the way out."

Adora tapped her chin. "If you can see the house, you should have access through the wards without the whole gut boiling problem."

Should wasn't exactly the word I wanted to hear when my guts were on the line.

"Isn't there a way I can test it without sacrificing my internal organs? I happen to be fond of those, preferably at body temperature."

"Nope. Once any part of you crosses the boundary, the wards will activate."

I nodded. "Of course they will." A bubble of nausea brewed in my stomach. The little house didn't look like it wanted to boil me from the inside. Patches of icy snow clung to the sides of the walkway. A light, earthy scent cleared away the bitter air of the rest of Reverence Square.

I bit my lip. I trusted Valen. He'd saved my life multiple times. If he wanted to hide his home from me, my subpar magical abilities wouldn't break through his wards. He wanted me to find this—he had to.

The alternative was boiled guts.

I stepped forward. A pulse of magic rubbed against me. The night was caught between winter and spring, but this icy touch only came from Valen's magic. It pulsed through me, sending a trail of tingles across my skin. I didn't stop. If boiling was in my future, I'd rather it happened quickly.

A little pop of relief flicked over me as I went through the wards. My heart hammered in my ears and my stomach clenched, waiting for a pain of heat.

Nothing. I'd done it.

"Woah," Krissa said. She reached her hand forward, feeling along the perimeter of the magic. "I can see the house now. That's incredible, and scary."

Adora and Ilene nodded in agreement.

"We should be able to enter the property now that Rae is giving us permission." She eyed me, and I nodded, just in case the wards needed to know I gave them permission.

"Maybe someone else can go first," Krissa suggested. "I mean, I love a good gut boiling as much as anyone, but I wouldn't mind an example to know how prepared to be."

Adora stepped off the street and onto the pathway. The magic flickered, but held, and she didn't double over in pain.

"It's okay, you guys can cross now."

But I'd already turned away from the others. A slight tug from inside the house pulled at the very center of my soul. I recognized the sensation and my heart sank instantly.

When a spellcaster died, any spells they'd cast previously disappeared, too—including protective wards. But Valen had given me some control over the wards around his house. If he died, my magic may sustain these wards.

The pull leading to Valen's house strengthened. My feet moved forward on their own, drawn and repelled by the same thing.

"Rae?" Krissa ran to my side. I turned to her, and whatever she saw on my face made her grab my hand. "What is it?"

I swallowed the lump in my throat. The thought of entering the house and confronting what may be inside ignited a swell of dread in my chest.

Please don't let it be him. Please. Please . . .

"Death," I said. "Something inside Valen's house is dead."

Chapter 9

Everything about the house was quiet. The door swung open without a sound. Cushioned rugs greeted our steps and silenced them immediately. Despite the empty fireplace, the interior was warm and . . . quiet.

Sparse furniture filled the space. A leather couch rested before the unlit fire. Two chairs and a table hugged the far wall, where the little kitchen wrapped around the corner. It smelled like Valen, evergreen, forest, and rain, which made my heart hurt more. Only two doors sat on the adjacent wall.

"That's the washroom." Adora pointed to the door closest to us. "And that's Valen's room."

I blinked. "Where's the guest room?"

"There isn't one. I crashed on the couch." She ran her hand over the couch and an odd look crossed her face. "I don't think I've actually seen Valen's room."

"That can't be right. When Valen healed me, he said I was in the guest room."

Adora shrugged. "Unless the man has a secret basement—which I wouldn't put it past him—there's only one bedroom in this house."

I wanted to linger in the living room. I wanted to see what the Nightwrath displayed on his walls, where he stored dishes in the cupboard, if a blanket pooled on the seat of the sofa. But an invisible string drew me toward that second door. It was both the tug of death and the need to confirm my new suspicion.

My hand hesitated over the knob. The rough wood concealed Valen's secrets. It might also hide his body.

A breath caught in my chest. What would I do if I opened the door and Valen was dead inside? The gaping jaws of fear stretched through my mind and sunk its sharpened fangs deep into my heart.

My hand shook. I couldn't do it. I couldn't open that door.

Someone's hand touched mine. The shock and warmth pulled me back enough to blink up at Ilene beside me.

"We'll do it together," she whispered.

There was fear in her eyes, too. She loved Valen, cared about him in a way I could never understand. She didn't want to find her brother's body, but standing here couldn't bring him back if he was gone.

I nodded. Her hand tightened over mine. Together, we turned the knob.

It didn't smell like death. It smelled so good. Springtime and earth and memories of Valen's skin pressing against mine. If I closed my eyes, he could be right next to me, ready to correct my fighting stance or brush a strand of hair from my face.

Darkness hid the vaulted ceilings that I remembered from my last trip here. But the black sheets across the dark wooden bed were the same. Moonlight filtered between the curtains and brushed over the light-colored walls.

He'd brought me *here*, into his own room, to tend my wounds.

I stepped inside and ran my fingertips along the silken sheet. He'd put me on his bed. Suddenly, the phantom memories of these sheets over my skin took on a far different flavor. Why had he lied about it being a guest room?

Rescuing Valen was the only way to find that answer.

Ilene let out a breath beside me. "He's not here." She sounded relieved, and I felt the same. That knot in my chest loosened a bit.

"No, he's not," I agreed, but that pull of death continued to pulse in my chest. "But something is still dead in the house."

"The Oracle," she whispered, her eyes widening. "That's why he used such powerful wards. He hid the Oracle of Faedor here."

I raised my brows. "The what?"

"The Oracle can prophesize potential futures. It's been lost for millennia, but Valen had managed to hunt it down. We need to use it to test strategies once the war begins. It's our only chance at gaining an advantage against Erline."

I had too many questions to ask while standing in Valen's bedroom. "Okay, I will need more information about all of that later. Right now, what are we looking for?"

"A severed head." Ilene didn't skip a beat.

But I did.

"... a ... what?"

She dropped to her knees, unflustered when her armor creaked in protest. "It's the severed head of a woman. Her mouth is open, and her tongue will be a little depressed in the center."

Ilene searched under Valen's bed as though browsing for any lost trinket, and not a severed head with a depressed tongue.

Krissa peeked around the corner. "Is he dead in there?"

"No," I said.

"Bummer." She stepped inside. "I mean, oh goodie."

"Shut up."

We both watched Ilene's search for a handful of seconds. She committed deeper beneath the bed frame, and her ass stuck up into the air.

Krissa's mouth dropped. Her face turned red.

I wrinkled my nose. Sure, Ilene's ass was great. It was a very nice shape, obviously strengthened by her regular battles, probably a little lumpy with all that armor she refused to take off. But it certainly wasn't worth the blush spreading across Krissa's face and down her neck.

Or was it? Was I unconsciously blushing? I pressed my fingers into my cheek. It felt normal.

I elbowed my friend, and she snapped out of her trance.

"I . . . sorry, what?"

"We're looking for a severed head."

She nodded. "Oh, okay, sure. Wait. What? A severed *what?*"

"A woman's severed head."

Krissa pointed to Ilene's ass, still bobbing in the air. "*That's* what she's looking for? Whose head is it? Did Valen kill someone?"

Ilene finally scooted back and sat on her heels. "My brother has killed many people. The Oracle of Faedor is not one of them. The woman was born with the Sight and wished to use her gift into eternity. A great necromancer granted her desire and preserved her power and flesh once the soul moved on."

"Okayyyyy." Krissa dragged the word out. "But why do we want it, though? We couldn't even see the house at all. Surely it's safer staying right where it is."

Ilene and I shared a glance. I knew the tightness around her mouth and eyes mirrored mine.

"It's likely these wards will only stand as long as my brother continues breathing."

I nodded. "If whoever took Valen decides it's easier just to kill him . . ." My throat tightened. I forced my voice to sound flat, normal, even as a scream tried to build in my chest. "The spells might fail, and the Oracle will be exposed."

"Hmm," Krissa responded. "But couldn't your magic keep the spells secure?"

"It's a risk we cannot take," Illene said.

"You just don't want to see the severed head, do you?" I crossed my arms and narrowed my eyes.

"Of course I don't. That sounds icky." Krissa pointed at Ilene again. "But if she says it's important for the freedom of the people, or whatever, then I believe her. I'll look for the severed head, but if I find it, I will throw up."

I smiled. Krissa looked like a too-big child with her arms on her hips and a scowl across her face. A plethora of colors wrapped from her hair to her socks, adding to the appearance of youth. My chest swelled with love. This annoying, selfless person was my best friend, and I wouldn't trade her for anything.

"Thanks," I said, trying to put all those feelings into the single word.

She blushed, and stuttered, retreating from the room without saying anything else.

When I turned to Ilene, she was watching where Krissa had been. A little pink stained her perfect cheeks.

Oh.

Oh . . .

"You like her," I blurted out.

"Of course I do. She unequivocally accepted my sudden appearance from a beam of light, dressed in battle-worn armor, and opened her home to me while I searched for my brother. What's not to like?"

"No, you like-*like* her."

Those blue eyes swiveled to me. An intensity I hadn't seen before filled the irises. I bet that's what Ilene looked like right before she relieved an enemy of their head.

But it wasn't enough to stop my stupid mouth.

"You have a crush on Krissa."

Ilene moved faster than should have been possible. One moment she crouched on the floor, the next her sword flashed in the moonlight as it aimed at me.

Our blades touched. My back hit the wall, but I didn't give Ilene's weapon an inch of room toward my throat.

Her brows creased as she assessed my defense. A swell of pride bubbled in my chest. She hadn't expected my block.

That intense gaze locked onto my face. She spoke casually, like we didn't have two swords crossed between our bare necks.

"You will not speak a word of this assumption to your friend."

I raised my brows. "This seems like an overreaction to this situation."

"It does not *feel* like one," she growled.

"I was just making an observation. You know, girl talk?"

She blinked, dark lashes framing her beautiful eyes. "Girl talk? I've never heard the phrase. It sounds . . . youthful."

"You've never heard . . . Nevermind, it doesn't matter. Girl talk is when girls get together to talk about things boys either wouldn't understand, or we don't want them to know. Being interested in certain people can fall into that category. Asking about your attraction to Krissa is girl talk. It's something friends do."

Ilene tilted her head. "Friends?"

Oh my. I had more work to do here than I expected.

"Here, how about we . . ." I gently pulled my blade down and pinched the tip of Ilene's so it wouldn't accidentally stab through my throat. She didn't react as I scooted away and shoved my weapon into its sheath. "There, that's better. Friends don't threaten each other at sword point." My face burned as I remembered when I trapped Valen inside a powerful ward and forced him to fight me when I'd learned he kept information from me. "Usually, at least."

Ilene sheathed her sword in an easy, graceful movement. "Are we . . . friends?"

"Sure." I shrugged. "I'm pretty new at this whole thing, too. But I think that only friends would search for severed heads together."

She smiled. It was small, tight, but there. Progress.

"I would like to be your friend. And later, I would like to engage in this *girl talk* again. I am having feelings toward that woman which I have not experienced in a long time. Maybe talking about it would . . . help."

I put my hand on Ilene's armored shoulder. "Absolutely. First, we find the Oracle of Faedor. Then, we talk about your crush on Krissa."

Chapter 10

The Oracle was better hidden than we'd expected.

I now knew what Valen displayed on his walls. Little paintings of tiny sunsets, the swell of a wave right before it crested at its point, and a silhouette of a woman standing against the sun, all shadows around the fading light. Valen didn't have many dishes in his cupboard. A matching goblet to the one Ilene scryed with earlier. The bare minimum of plates, bowls, and cooking equipment. He did, in fact, have one wool blanket pooled on the seat of the couch. When I sucked in a breath when no one was looking, it smelled like moss and pine trees.

But the severed head was still hiding.

Bubbles and Whiskers curled together on the empty cushions. Their noses touched, each snoring softly against the other. I clutched the blanket tighter. I wanted Valen's warmth beside me while Bubbles slept. Together, and safe.

"I'll have to leave soon." Adora flopped onto the ground, apparently reluctant to reclaim the couch, and reclined her head into both hands. "It's still not safe for me to go out and about during the day."

Krissa yawned. "I have a class tomorrow, too."

I pressed my lips together in frustration. The house contained one bedroom, a washroom, and a combined kitchen and living area. We'd torn them all apart, flipping the mattress and couch over to check for secret compartments and any hinges leading to a concealed basement. I'd only found dust and too many hidden daggers to count.

The pull was still there. My magic felt the Oracle, but we couldn't find it.

Ilene turned to me. "We need you to find it."

"I don't know how. I can feel there's something dead in this house, but I haven't practiced my power in years."

"Sit down." She put both hands on my shoulder and sank me onto the arm of the couch. "Now close your eyes."

I obliged with a sigh but had little hope of any of her directives actually working.

"Don't sigh at me. This is what I used to do with Valen when his power emerged."

My eyes fluttered open again. "Really? How old was he?" I tried to imagine Ilene and Valen as children, but the images refused to come. They could only be the strong, imposing figures I knew them as now.

"Let's just say Valen came into his gifts later in life. Close your eyes again."

I did. Eliminating my sight brought forth both Valen's scent and that pull from my soul.

"Reach out with the barest bit of your magic."

I tensed. "If I use my magic, the King of Erline will know my location."

"Shhh. I'm not asking you to use the magic. Just touch it, recognize it. Every power has an active and passive ability. You're able to passively instill sentience into other objects. You should be able to feel similar types of magic."

I hadn't really wanted Adora to know the specifics of my power, but I bit my tongue. Maybe it didn't matter anymore. If war was about to be on our doorsteps, Adora and I would be on the same team.

With an exhale, I let the tendril of my powers spread through the house. I didn't linger in the places where Valen's magic had recently touched. I wanted to. The power ached to wallow in the shallows that tasted of him. I forced it to move on, to follow the tug and pull of the feel of death.

I lost sight of the house. The shape became meaningless as the lines of magic strengthened in my mind. I could see the ley-lines that streaked through the ground as little rivers of pure magic. Echoes of Valen's wards traced beneath the foundation to protect all sides of his property.

Amongst the other powers, death spoke to me.

I stood from the couch. Part of me recognized the hushed whispers that ensued. Mostly, though, I ignored them as I reached for death.

Comfort, peace, it whispered in my ears. *Calm, quiet, rest . . .*

Ah, so tempting. Most people saw death as vile or evil. They ran from it, cried when it claimed a loved one's life. It's true that death was permanent, but it was also compassionate. Death soothed aches and pains, brought about impossible peace, and delivered rest. Terrible and awesome was the song it sang to me.

I followed that melody through Valen's house. The pull didn't lead me to the bedroom, as I originally thought, but to the space between the washroom and bedroom doors.

My eyes snapped open, and I crouched down. Cold wood ran along my skin as I trailed my fingertips over the surface of the wall. A little edge danced against my hand—almost imperceivable.

"It's here," I said. "This used to be a small door. Valen sealed it."

We hadn't thought to look in the damn *walls*.

Ilene didn't question my discovery. She pulled her sword out and ordered a stark, "stand back."

I'd barely shuffled away when the heavy broadsword smashed into the wall. Krissa released a little shriek as dust and mortar flaked through the air like snowfall.

When the dust settled, the Oracle of Faedor perched in the space.

She was . . . cute. Raven hair swirled around the face to pool along the golden platter the head perched on. Her eyes were open, narrow and staring out at us with an unseeing gaze. Most shocking were the painted red lips, parted wide, her pink tongue folded in the center.

Krissa angled to see around my shoulder.

"Hm," she said. "I expected it to be more . . . severed."

The bottom edges of the neck where the skin should touch the torso were smooth and flat. It looked less hacked and more carefully flayed.

"Why isn't it talking or anything?" Adora asked.

"The Oracle of Faedor can only be awoken by placing a very specific stone into its mouth." Ilene stuck her finger into the gaping hole, followed by several groans of disgust, including my own. "It will rest here, and the Oracle will speak the future once more."

"What stone is it?"

Ilene shrugged. "Little is known about the stone, or the Oracle, actually. Valen spent years researching before finally discovering their locations while serving time in Erline's dungeons. Information is traded easily for food and water in such a pitiful place."

My gut clenched. "I didn't know Valen had been imprisoned at the capital." I'd walked the dungeon halls throughout my youth. Often accompanied by the other Providers as they chose which prisoners' lives I would steal to pass onto the king.

"He wouldn't have mentioned it." A shiver crept up Ilene's spine. "It was a dark time for my brother."

And it clearly bothered her as well. Perhaps it was her orders that brought Valen into the dungeons in the first place. I bit my tongue. The pile of questions I prepared for the mercenary grew longer with each day it took us to find him.

"We need to leave now if I want to return to my hideout before sunrise." Adora stood, clearing space for the rest of us to follow. "Where is the safest place to hide the Oracle?"

"My house." I pulled the head on its golden platter from the hole in the wall. "Valen knows my wards are strong. He made sure that if he ever disappeared, I'd be able to find his house and protect the Oracle." As much as I wished he'd allowed me into his house for deeper feelings, I knew this was the real reason.

Ilene seemed less convinced. She crossed her arms and studied me. "What are these wards?"

"Well, I haven't tested them yet, but the current one is called Fire-Crotch. You're welcome to determine if it's up to your standards or not."

She bit her lip. "That actually sounds fine to me."

I was tired. Lingering in Valen's empty home only exhausted me further. The ache in my chest pounded in beat with my heart. He was gone. *Thump.* I couldn't find him. *Thump.* What if it was too late? *Thump, thump, thump.*

We walked toward the door. The motion woke the sleeping warplog and hoglet, both of whom jumped from the couch with their respective groans.

Bubbles took two hops before looking up at me with his beady, little eyes. They refocused on the tray in my hand and widened. Little green circles of acid drool collected in the corners of his mouth.

"No." I pulled the tray higher. "This is not for you."

A shine danced over the warplog's eyes.

"Stop it."

His lipless mouth started stretching open. I groaned. The warplog didn't stop widening his maw, exposing rows of ragged and sharp teeth. Hot, rancid drool bubbled in the pit of his throat. Bubbles' mouth opened larger than his little body, larger than should be physically possible.

Ilene screeched.

"Krissa!" I yelled. My hands were full of what Bubbles had deemed a delicious looking snack.

"On it!"

She sprinted to the warplog and firmly gripped his jaws, forcing them back together. His mouth shrunk slowly back to normal. The acid drool stopped dripping on the floor. He looked at me and blinked, essentially crying in warplog language.

"I just fed you," I told him. "And you can't eat the magic head. We need it."

He kept his mouth shut, but still looked sad as everyone trailed out of Valen's house and into the night.

I spared one glance back. Next time I entered that house, I vowed Valen would be there with me.

Chapter 11

Ilene swiveled to me.

"Maybe the Oracle should not stay at your house." She eyed Bubbles. "The warplog may consume it."

It was hard to argue with that. Bubbles would happily eat the head.

"There's no safer place for it."

"Perhaps—"

Adora threw her hand up and interrupted Ilene's thought.

"Shh!" We hushed immediately. "Do you hear that?"

Sounds of faraway fires, voices, and laughter filtered to us. Forest noises of tiny feet along trees and the rustle of leaves blended into the calmness of the night. Everything sounded normal.

Krissa tapped my arm. "Rae, look at these." She pointed into the snow at the end of Valen's property line.

Overlapping sets of a shoe print ran right beyond the boundaries of the wards. I knelt and studied the rounded shape. It was the same distinct impression repeated.

"Someone's been walking here," I murmured.

"It's not illegal to walk down the street." Adora crossed her arms, but her hurried glances said her attention was not on the footwear patterns in the snow.

"This isn't just walking. The owner of these shoes paced across the property line right here. Krissa, hand me your shoe."

She shrugged off one shoe without a question. It took a moment to juggle the severed head in one hand and a shoe in the other, but I lifted the sole toward the silvered moonlight.

Tiny silver nails danced in the night. "These are the places where the cobbler attached the leather to the edge of the shoe. And these grooves are cut into the leather to allow for traction. But no cobbler can make the exact same pattern twice." I set Krissa's shoe in the snow and pressed down. "This is what her shoes look like."

Adora scanned the snow and pointed. "Right here. This pattern matches that shoe."

"Exactly. Now study the sequencing of the new footprints we're seeing."

Ilene's voice came first. "They're on top of ours."

"Yes, they are. Which means someone paced along this perimeter after we'd gone onto Valen's property. Is there anything else different about the new tracks compared to Krissa's shoe?"

"There are holes in the center?"

"Exactly. The holes are called studs, and soldiers have them embedded in the bottom of the leather soles to give more grip into the ground during fighting. Whoever walked here was prepared for some kind of fight."

Adora crossed her arms. "But why would they pace here? Nobody can see Valen's house except you."

I pressed my lips. A sinking weight in my gut told me I already knew the answer.

"They watched us go through the wards," Krissa said my fears aloud. "They couldn't see Valen's house themselves, but they knew the approximate location. If they knew the Oracle was inside . . ."

Damn it.

Krissa had connected the dots before I did. I leapt to my feet, only will and luck preventing the head from tumbling off its platter.

"They were waiting for us to leave," I said.

Silence crept along the street. My heart roared in my ears. Anyone could watch us from behind the trees or nearby structures, and they'd be almost invisible.

A slow clap from slightly behind us broke the silence. A shadow stepped out from the depths of the neighbor's house. The person's black outfit consumed the moonlight and smothered any hints of identification. They were lengthy and slim and held a chain in one hand, which rattled eerily with each strike of their clapping.

Leisurely, the newcomer lifted one hand and pointed at me.

Damn it all to hell.

I didn't have time to plead for a respite from the universe. Adrenaline flooded my veins and turned off any unnecessary part of my mind. Get the Oracle to safety. Keep everyone alive. That was all that mattered.

"Run!" Ilene and I screamed at the same time.

Adora grabbed Krissa's hand, who seemed to have trouble processing the imminent danger before us. The two streaked down the street.

Ilene glanced back at me. "Get the Oracle out of here."

"I can't leave you here." I wanted to draw my sword, but running with the platter and the weapon would be impossible.

Her sword flashed in the moonlight as she spun it. "If we lose that Oracle, Valen's sacrifice will be meaningless." A smile stained her mouth white. "Besides, if the king's soldiers haven't killed me yet, I doubt this little wisp will."

The 'little wisp' decided our head start was up. They sprinted at Ilene, all shadows and speed, and the whip flicked out lightning fast. Ilene laughed as it touched her sword, and her nimble body eased from its reach effortlessly.

I took a moment to pick my jaw up from the ground. If that strike had aimed at me, I'd have to kiss my head goodbye. Ilene moved like she knew exactly where the whip would land.

With one more sharp word from the Phoenix Queen, I gripped the platter tight and ran.

Running sucked. My lungs tried to turn into lead bricks. The platter shifted my center of gravity and slowed my strides. One rogue rock would take me straight down onto the cobblestone street.

Someone screamed ahead.

The sound should have persuaded me to go a different direction. The Oracle in my hands was the most important thing to protect if we wanted Ilene's rebellion to have any chance of success. A good soldier made sacrifices for the betterment of the whole.

Yeah. I wasn't a soldier, much less a *good* one. And I was pretty sure the high-pitched scream belonged to Krissa. I'd use the Oracle's head as a cannonball before I let anything happen to my best friend.

I forced my feet to move faster. My burning sides and heaving breaths faded into the back of my mind. Magic twisted in my core, spurred by the thrill of the night. Krissa screamed again. The sound abruptly cut off.

I ran harder.

Chapter 12

The road opened into a wider intersection. We'd been pushed along the narrow pathway between Reverence Square and The Void.

The Void had once sprawled uninterrupted across the majority of Hallow's Promise. When the city walls went up, people hacked down the massive trees and slaughtered the terrifying creatures. Most of The Void retreated. But one small section remained in the upper corner of town. Mysterious beings and magical impossibilities occurred inside The Void and no amount of civilized development seemed to reign in that particular area.

Krissa and Adora squared off against a second veiled figure. This one was bulkier, more masculine in the span of the shoulders and width of their thighs. He fought with a pointed weapon that resembled the cross between a sword and an ice pick.

He saw my approach and abruptly shrugged away from Adora's strike, aiming toward me. Luckily, Adora moved faster, her dagger swinging into an arc toward his back. The man paused to deflect the strike and Krissa used the moment to sprint to me.

I grabbed her with my free arm. Her chest heaved, but she

appeared unharmed.

"Are you ok?"

Krissa nodded. "He cut us off from the trees. I think I screamed, but I don't really remember."

"Listen to me." I squeezed her arm harder until her shocked expression wore away and she focused on my face. I gently pressed the platter into her hands. "I need you to take this and run into The Void."

She did a slow blink. "No."

"Okay, 'no' isn't really an option right now. Adora handles her blade well enough, but this guy is obviously a trained fighter. He is going to beat her eventually, and your back will be exposed."

But Krissa shook her head. "I can't carry that. No way. It's gross."

"*That's* what's bothering you? The head is not gross. Just . . . think about how proud Ilene will be if you protect the Oracle for her."

A spark lit in her eye. "Proud?"

"Of course. She'll probably compliment your bravery. Maybe she'll give you a hug out of gratitude."

"A hug?"

I nodded and pressed the platter into her grip again. "Go ahead. Prove to your girlfriend that you can do hard things."

"She's not my girlfriend," Krissa murmured, but she accepted the head.

"Now, go hide in The Void."

"What's your plan after that?"

"Define 'plan.'"

"The chronological sequence of events that are determined prior to the initiation of the first one."

Yikes. "It's not really a plan. More of a rough estimate. Maybe a little bit of hope thrown in."

She sighed. "I was afraid you'd say that."

Adora cried out. The man lifted his arm again, landing a harsh strike against her block. Her shaky return and slouching stance meant she was tiring.

"I've got to go." I ran before Krissa moved. I trusted her. She would go into The Void even if she was worried that something with big teeth might take a little chomp.

When the attacker moved toward Adora again, my blade smashed against his. Tendrils of smoke oozed from the metal and cascaded around both of us.

"It'ssss you," the man hissed from behind a fabric face covering. Some of his consonants slipped together and dragged out the sound. "You are the one we've been looking for."

I pushed my sword into his ice pick weapon, and he stumbled backward. "Congratulations, you've found me. As a reward, you get to eat dirt." I placed my foot in the center of his chest and kicked him down. The man rolled smoothly and popped onto his feet.

Oh yeah, I was out of my league.

The wisps of smoke from my sword continued to billow around us. It thickened like fog clinging to our skin and clothing. Visibility thinned to just me and my opponent. All color faded from the world, leaving us trapped in a cloud of gray, impenetrable with a regular gaze.

"You ssssearch for the Nightwrath." His words were flat. A statement, not a question.

But they were sharp enough to gouge my heart.

"What do you know about Valen? Where is he?'

The man laughed. He circled me and I followed, keeping him

close.

"My bossss isss taking good care of your friend. No need to worry."

My palm ached where the guards at the base of the sword hilt dug into my skin. The irritation meant I gripped the weapon too tight, too close. But I couldn't force my fingers to relax. Letting emotions rule the fight led to failure. Even with Tyfin and Valen's voices saying that in my head, I only wanted to pummel the hilt into this man's face. I wished I could strangle him from here.

The smoke tendrils moved an inch closer to his neck.

I froze. I knew the attacker shifted, preparing for his next rally, but my mind tried to reconcile with what my eyes observed.

The smoke . . . had definitely moved closer to the guy's throat.

I ducked down and to the side. His pointy weapon dove over my head and oozed through the air. It left his gut exposed—which should have been an easy slash to part his skin down the center.

But I held my strike. I needed to know if the intentionality of the moving smoke was only my imagination. I'd been up all night. Someone I cared for deeply was missing. Two people tried to attack me and my friends. I'd carried a severed head on a platter.

Imagining that the smoke responded to my mental wishes was to be expected at this point.

As the man prepared his next movement, I envisioned a thick tendril of mist wrapping around his wrist. The shadows danced and swayed, and one lazy tentacle reached out to touch his hand.

I basically jumped to my feet.

"Did you see that?" I pointed to the smoke with my sword.

His brows creased.

"Oh, I guess you weren't looking. Here, I'll try again." I stuck my tongue against the back of my teeth. My brows clenched and my nose crinkled.

But the smoke *moved*. It coiled over the man's skin, licking up and down like he was a human-shaped lollipop. At first, he just stared at me, but as the mist solidified and turned from wispy clouds to solid bindings, he started screaming.

As I concentrated on the smoke, the current of magic streaming around me clarified. The power tasted like me, but was also its own. Little lines connected me to the misty fog, but also to the sword in my hand. I flipped the blade over, but both sides of the ornately carved metal looked the same as always.

I pulled on the wisps, and they consumed more of the man's arms. He yelled and bucked, but I put more strength into the tug and his arm froze upright.

I did the same with his legs. The man fell to the dirt at my knees.

"Oh hell, yes. Did you see *that*? I did that. All by myself." I swore the sword pulsed slightly in my hand. "Well, maybe I had some help. But still, that's totally badass. Nightwrath, huh? You know what? Call *me* Nightwrath now because I just handed you your butt."

"Rae?" Footsteps echoed through the dark. Ilene's face sharpened in the moonlight.

"Ilene! Come here, you have to see this!"

The woman slowed as she neared me and raised her brows. "See what?"

"What do you mean? Look . . ." I gestured toward my captive, but the space was empty.

All the thrill deflated immediately.

"He . . . he was just here . . ."

Ilene tapped her finger on her chin. "Did the sword create smoke again?"

"How did you . . . never mind. Yes, it did."

"And you were able to control the smoke?"

"Yes . . ."

"But then you got excited?"

"Maybe."

"And took your attention away from your fight?"

"Only because you showed up!"

Ilene patted my hand. "Smoke Wielding is a fickle skill. One brief moment of distraction and the smoke is happy to return to its natural state—nothing. But good job recognizing the potential. Sometimes it can take years to meld the smoke."

"I've never heard of Smoke Wielding." The blade looked so normal, but I felt the buzz that Ilene and Krissa must have experienced earlier. It vibrated softly in my hand, singing a melody just for me.

"I hadn't either, until Valen returned from Erline's captivity and had the ability to manipulate the smoke. He can create his own now, spurred from his magic. I imagine it's your sentient sword creating the smoke for you, or else Erline's king would be at your doorstep."

"The sword did that?"

"I believe so. It has its own power now that you've given it some kind of life. Both that life and power will continue to strengthen as long as you're close enough to siphon your magic into it."

I pressed my lips together. It was too late with too little sleep for these kinds of life altering reveals. "What happened with you?"

"My opponent also fled. Adora doubled back to collect the warplog and the hoglet. I believe she said to meet at the wagon in The Boid, but I could be wrong."

"The Void," I corrected. "Brew is here?"

Ilene nodded. "Adora said it showed up exactly when they needed it."

My heart swelled with pride. I loved that wagon.

Chapter 13

Suzie used to hate me, and sometimes when she glanced over her shoulder with that sharpened look in her eyes to send me a heated glare, I was sure she sort of still did.

"Yes, Rae, I am crushing the hyssop like the recipe says, not chopping it." She punctuated the statement with an eye roll.

I lightly smiled. Last time she'd tried to brew a difficult recipe, black sludge had exploded and covered my entire living room. It took Suzie days to scrub it all off the walls and floor.

I kept silent as I watched her work. She moved confidently inside the tight confines of Brew's interior. The wagon snapped cupboards open and closed as she reached for the ingredients to the potion the customer had ordered. A rich smell of sweet and earthy peppered the space. Fine beginnings of springtime sprinkled through the open sash and teased us with sunlight and a warming breeze.

We hadn't found Valen. A severed head rested in Brew's highest cabinet. Putting a preserved severed head anywhere near food preparation would probably be frowned upon by the Magical Consumption Committee. But they weren't here. Thankfully, Bubbles hadn't tried to eat her yet. I'd been unable to control the smoke again, or even conjure a wisp from my sword.

Things certainly weren't going great. In fact, if I was honest with myself, they downright sucked. I'd failed in every attempt to seek out Valen's location. If I had any part of him, I could use a tracking spell to pinpoint his location, but the man flickered in and out of my life like a shadow at sunset. He left nothing personal behind.

I tore my gaze from Suzie's work and cradled my head in my hand. I didn't usually sit inside Brew—too busy cutting, chopping, crushing, stirring, or any number of tasks required to create the crafted tonics and potions our customers craved. But today, I'd pulled out a stool and collapsed onto it, wishing I could snore as loudly as Bubbles.

"Alright, I'm ready for the magic." Suzie wiped her hands on her apron and smiled back at me. Her expression faded when she saw my face. Hm, guess I wasn't keeping it together as well as I thought.

"Go ahead," I said softly. "You know what to do."

She refocused on the beverage. Magic bristled around me, hot and bright. Suzie had a unique blend of power I'd never seen before. I could only train her to a certain point, but soon she'd need a more advanced teacher specific to her type of magic.

The little lavender-colored drink sat unassuming in front of her. I'd named the beverage BREW-licious Lavender. It's herbal tea foundation with splashes of citrus and a light, magical boost oozed calmness and relaxation.

Maybe I'd have Suzie make me a cup, too.

She hunched over the counter. I couldn't see her face, but imagined her eyes were closed as she concentrated on the power. The magic flexed with her demand, thick and warm against me. I felt as she manipulated it. Heaviness settled over my skin. Tendrils of magic split from the horde and siphoned into the tea.

Suzie relaxed. She turned back to me with a big smile. "I did it."

I returned the expression. "Good job."

She handed the drink through the sash, and the rattle of coins followed the exchange. I leaned my back against Brew and closed my eyes. I swear the wood softened behind my body as Brew comforted me the best way it knew how.

"Maybe we should wrap up early. You fought off an attacker last night."

When I opened my eyes, Suzie's warm gaze studied me. I wondered what she saw. Was the defeat so obvious on my face? Could she see the panic as time stretched longer and our chances of finding Valen slimmed?

"I can't." Were the only words I allowed to tumble out of my mouth. Describing the burning ache in my chest or the way tears wanted to bunch along my lashes whenever I had a moment to think felt too heavy to discuss. "I don't have anything to do at home. Sitting alone . . . I can't do that right now."

"You could ask my dad for help."

I shook my head. "He doesn't care that Valen is missing. Besides, he and the sheriff are managing their own investigation."

"Doesn't seem like they're having any better luck." Suzie lowered her voice. "But Dad cares about *you*, Rae. He'll do anything for you."

I bit my tongue. That was almost worse. Leof did care for me, and I loved him, too—but I didn't know if I loved him the way he wished I did.

"Suzie . . ."

A scream erupted from outside the wagon.

We froze, our eyes locked on each other. Suzie's eyes widened as her expression changed from worried to alarmed. Brew flung open the rear door, and another scream pulsed through the morning air.

"Help! Someone help!"

I didn't usually show up during the plea for aid. The people my skills helped tended to be ice cold and dead still—literally. But my heart flopped in my chest as Suzie and I bolted for the open door.

The few customers queueing for the wagon glanced around for some kind of authority figure. Apparently, me and Suzie—the owner of the traveling tea shop and a woman barely old enough to attend the college across the street—looked adequately official that nobody else hurried toward the cries.

A woman stood in the middle of the street. She held both hands out from her body and the vivid splash of red was visible on her palms.

Blood.

She yelled out again, her plea broken on the last syllable. Suzie sprinted ahead of me, and I swear a faint yellow glow emitted from her hands. Hopefully our practice with her magic would maintain her control. I didn't want to put out any forest fires if she decided to start chucking balls of light in a panic.

As we neared, the sharp features of the woman clarified. She had short, cropped hair pulled into a messy twist at the top of her head. Dark brows rimmed her wide eyes. Recognition made me stumble. It was Elo—the customer who had noticed my sword smoking when I sold her some tea.

I grabbed her arms, ignoring the blood on her palms, and scanned her body. No other red marred her clothes or skin.

She wasn't injured, but her arms felt cold.

"What's wrong?" I tried to steady my voice. The cool skin was a textbook symptom for shock, and I needed Elo to remain calm and answer my questions.

"I—He—Over there!" She flung one arm free from my grip and pointed deeper into the woods along the edge of the street. "I tried to help, but . . ." Her words faded, and tears rimmed her bottom lashes. She went back to studying her palms, as though the crimson liquid explained everything she couldn't say.

I pulled her into a tight embrace. I wasn't much of a hugging person—especially with a stranger I barely knew—but tight pressure could help manage some symptoms of the shock.

"I was too late," she whispered into my ear. The sobs she'd held back spilled over the dam, and she sucked in a hard breath that released as a loud cry.

Damn it. I wasn't good with crying people.

"Suzie, I need you to take care of Elo. She's going into shock. Take her to Brew—" Crap, I had an illegal severed head in the cupboard, which I couldn't risk her seeing. "And put the stool in the sunshine to warm her up. Make a really hot tea. Nothing fancy —quick is better than good. Chamomile or Willow's bark for calming."

After Suzie wrapped her arm around Elo and I watched them wander safely toward the wagon, I turned to where Elo pointed into the woods.

My tongue stuck to the roof of my mouth, and I drew my sword. That strange buzz tingled against my fingertips, but I didn't let it distract me.

The forest was quiet today. The warm air should have encouraged chirping birds and chippy squirrels to meander through the canopy. Instead, a hush spread along the tree line. Shadows flickered and danced as the late winter sun played through the leaves—as eerie as a phantom.

My steps broke through the hush. Branches snapped along my soles. I didn't want to be silent—I wanted to confront whatever threat lay here as quickly as possible. A breeze, smelling of flowers and river water, carried the sounds before me.

But nobody heard them.

Only a handful of steps through the tree line led me to the place where Elo had pointed to. A little pocket through the brush opened wide enough to allow three or four people to comfortably stand and remain concealed from any casual passersby on the street. A man lay on his back in the center of the space, blood trailing from his lips and eyes.

Ah, finally something I could use my skills for, as the man was very much dead.

Chapter 14

Leof crouched beside me. His constables milled around the trees, searching for any additional evidence other than the dead man on the ground. When I first accepted the role of Crime Investigation Expert, the constables hated listening to my directions. They'd get angry when I asked them to maintain a wider perimeter around the body. They bickered when I told them not to touch the decedent to avoid the possibility of contaminating lingering scent maps.

Most of them were used to me by now. It turned out that they all liked solving crimes and keeping Hallow's Promise safe. When it became apparent that my techniques helped with those goals, they started smiling and joking with me, and—most importantly—listening to me.

Except for Castor.

The constable crossed his arms and looked down his pointed nose at me. "There aren't any significant wounds on the body. There's no indication that this was a crime. He has bags of illegal substances in his pockets—he probably took one too many and his body gave out."

I tightened my fingers into fists. The sharpness of my nails dug into my skin and the sensation helped me focus.

"How many instances of substance overuse have you been

to, Castor?" There, my voice sounded perfectly calm and level and not at all as pissed as the boiling anger inside my chest felt.

He snorted. "More than you."

"And how many had the victim bleeding from external orifices?"

There was a pulse of silence. "It could be something new."

"Or it could be murder. Now please shut up and get away from my body."

Castor moved while murmuring under his breath, but I knew he wouldn't go far. He'd be ready to pounce as soon as I stepped away from Leof.

Tension between the werewolf and I still bristled. I had a million things I wanted to say, none of which were appropriate while standing beside a dead man. His lips pressed tight, exposing a little dimple on one side. He smelled good, a little earth and old leather combined.

"Tell me what you see, Rae."

I was sure Leof didn't want a report of how his sharpened jaw cut into a square chin that I knew was a comfortable place to rest my head. Nor did he want to know that the top button of his uniform was undone and offering the smallest peak of his strong chest.

No, he wanted to hear about the body.

The man rested supine on the ground. Some debris from the trees and wind had brushed over his face and stuck to the blood along his eyes and mouth. Smears of red touched his neck and chest—where Elo had tried to persuade him to breathe. Even more of the liquid trailed out of his nose and ears. He wore a black coat, which was filled to the brim with illegal hallucinogenic herbs and tonics.

I didn't mind the dead. Tending to them this way allowed

one more act of kindness while they remained in this world. I had a job to do, and I was good at it. But I didn't like every part.

I hated their faces the most.

His eyelids were half closed, staring at the world he no longer saw. The jaw slacked as rigor hadn't set in yet. His mouth and tongue looked foreign, too pale and blue to belong to a human body.

But I made myself look at him—at every detail. It wasn't pretty, but life wasn't pretty, either. The truth was, I would carry his memory in my mind. Long after I forgot his name, I would remember his face. I carved out a piece of this world for the man whose life was taken unfairly at the expense of a piece of myself.

Which, of course, wasn't what Leof was asking for either.

"He has very few wounds. There isn't anything apparent that would cause his death." I gently picked up one of the stranger's hands. Fine red lines crossed along his skin. "These look like defensive wounds, so there was probably a struggle. There are some larger ones along his biceps, and the fabric is slashed, too."

"What about the contraband?"

I shook my head. "I don't think it's related. If someone, or something, killed him for that, why leave everything in his pockets?"

"Castor thinks he took too much of his own supply."

"Castor's an idiot."

"I agree. But what do you think?"

I sat back on my heels. "Look at this swelling along the neck and chest." I outlined the areas with my fingertips. His skin was hard, unyielding. Mulched patterns of red and purple peppered the raised areas. "This isn't what I expect from decomposition in such a short time or caused by any sort of bladed weapon that could create those other scratches."

"Which means . . ."

"It looks like an allergic reaction."

Leof blinked. "A swarm of bees didn't kill him, Rae. And I don't think any amount of pollen could cause that." He gestured to all the blood.

I shrugged. "Alivia can give her expert opinion. I'm just qualified to make observations."

"Do you want to know what I think?"

"Sure."

But Leof didn't answer. When I looked up, the wolf stared at me, flecks of gold in his amber eyes. Heated intensity locked on my face and burned into my chest.

"I think you've been looking for Valen after I told you not to."

My throat tightened. "You *asked* me not to."

"I told you it was dangerous, and you were going to get hurt. Last night, one of my guys got a report of two separate altercations in Reverence Square. Do you know anything about that?"

"Define 'anything.'"

Leof cursed. "The Sheriff and I are investigating the disappearances. You're only going to stir up more trouble."

First, I was a little insulted that he wasn't impressed with the trouble I'd already stirred up. Also, a flicker of anger burst into life at the implication that nothing I did would actually be helpful.

But all of that melted away when I looked back at the body on the ground.

"You think this man was attacked by the same person who took Valen?" The world narrowed.

"Of course, I do. This man's name was Pomplo Trevador Barlin, and he smuggled illicit substances into Hallow's Promise and sold them to the smaller criminals for public distribution. His image is on the forbidden list at both gates into the city, but he passes in and out without a problem. He's either bribing the guards or has a secret way through the walls. He's the exact type of target our perpetrator has been kidnapping."

My sword lurched in its sheath, and I agreed with it. Whoever took Valen had been in this clearing, yards away from Brew, and I hadn't noticed a thing. If I'd been here moments earlier, I could have found them. I would have forced them to tell me where Valen was.

Leof's touch on my shoulder drew me away from the rage. "Can they take the body to the morgue, or do you need more time?"

I *needed* to stab something with the pointy part of my sword.

"They can take the body. I'll go to the morgue in the morning and see what Alivia finds."

Leof held out a hand to help me up, and I accepted. He pulled me to my feet with ease, but his touch lingered on my skin.

"I'm sorry he's missing, Rae."

I turned and started walking away. "No, you're not."

He caught me easily. "I am sorry that you're hurting. That wasn't my intention when I told you to stay away from this investigation. I just wanted to—"

"Keep me safe, I know." I ground my teeth until my jaw hurt. "But I can keep myself safe, Leof. This man, Pomplo, he . . ." The sobs tried to fight out of my chest, but I sucked them deep inside my body, where the memories of my life in Erline also hid. I gestured toward the two constables now picking up the body. "This could have been Valen. It still might be."

Leof's eyes softened. "I'm sorry, Rae. No more secrets. I'll help you find him. I promise."

That hurt, too. I had secrets Leof could never discover. Ilene, the rebellion, my supposed role to play that even I didn't know.

I turned away from him and studied the ground to hide my guilt.

A familiar impression settled in the shallow dirt beneath my feet.

I gasped. Leof froze, his hand immediately aiming for his sword as he searched for some perceived threat.

"It's the same footprint," I whispered.

He stepped beside me and looked at the mark in the ground. "The same as . . . what?"

"The print potentially involved in the incident at Reverence Square last night. I need to make a cast. Hand me those big rocks over there."

Leof compiled without question, and I stacked the rocks in a little square as an indicator to avoid stepping in the area.

"So, whoever attacked you in the Square also killed this man?"

"I never said I was there last night."

"Rae."

"Based on my skills and experience, yes, the same people involved in said altercation—which I know nothing about—appear to be involved here, too."

Leof ran a hand over his face. He looked tired. "You know that you're getting dangerously close to filling in all the boxes these perpetrators target, right?"

My brows creased. "What do you mean? I'm not a criminal."

"You're suspiciously close to the most dangerous mercenary

in town and you hang out at the Siren's Sorrow. Having access to the underground circles makes you good at your job, but from the outside, it looks a lot like canoodling."

"I've never canoodled a day in my life." But I chewed on his words in my mind. Maybe the key to finding Valen was to have the kidnappers take me straight to him. I filed the possibility away in my mind as a last resort.

"All you ever do is canoodle." Castor crunched through the twigs. "They should change your title to Crime Canoodle Expert. It would be a more accurate title for your smoke and mirror techniques."

Little did he know my smoke could strangle the life from his body. If I could figure out how to use it . . .

"What do you want?" I snapped.

"I'm not here for you, witch. Marshal, the sheriff is on scene. He wants to talk to you."

Chapter 15

Sheriff Jean was a very tall man. We'd only officially met one time, and he told me to call him Jean, so I didn't know his full name. Most people said 'the sheriff' and left it at that. The four-letter name was far too short for a man of his intimidating stature. He towered over Leof, which was hard to do, and lines of muscles flexed beneath the dark brown sheriff's uniform. The gold emblem of Erline formed a badge on his chest.

He held his hand out to me as a greeting. "Shay, right?"

I returned the gesture. "Rae, actually."

"Of course, of course. Sorry about that. I've been traveling from the capital so much with these investigations." He waved his hand. "It's wearing me out, quite honestly. Ah, Marshal. Tell me, what do we have here?"

Leof stepped up. "The man's body was found shortly after he died by an . . . Elo Hamerton Gloude. She tried resuscitation for several minutes before giving up and calling for help. The scene appears as clean as the rest."

"You think it's the same perps?"

"It's following similar patterns. The only difference is this guy ended up dead. They're bringing the body to the morgue."

Sheriff Jean's gaze snapped to where two constables wrapped the dead man in a white sheet to make transporting the body a little easier.

His face sharpened.

"Naw, don't bother with that."

Leof tensed. "With what, sir?"

"Don't bother bringing Barlin to the mortician. We don't need to waste her time."

I blinked and avoided the temptation to clean out my ears. Surely the sheriff wasn't suggesting that this man's death wasn't worthy of a thorough investigation.

"Sir." Leof's voice was careful. "It's standard procedure for all murder victims to be examined by the mortician."

Sheriff Jean snorted. "I'd hardly call this piece of criminal trash a victim, Leof. You said the scene was clean. I can't imagine what we'd learn from his body that we don't already know. Let the man find some rest—and you, too. You should sleep good tonight knowing one more dealer is off the streets."

Jean apparently didn't know Leof very well. The marshal put everything into his cases. He didn't care if the victims were composed of the very scum of the earth—justice reigned supreme. Regardless of status—Pomplo or the wealthiest person living in the Chopines—the victims were given the same respect and dedication for their cases. It was something I strongly admired in the werewolf.

But Jean didn't notice. "Let's talk to the girl, huh? I'd like to get out of here before sunrise."

I pressed my lips together to avoid saying something insulting. The sheriff paid my bills and held sway over Leof's life. Friends aren't supposed to make life more difficult, so it was better to keep my complaints quiet—for now.

Elo sat on a large rock at the edge of the guarded perimeter of the scene. She wrapped both hands around a little mug that she stared into without lifting to her lips. Suzie sat beside the woman and settled one arm around her slim shoulders. Elo looked up as we approached.

"Hello, ma'am. I'm the local sheriff, but you can call me Jean—everyone does. I'd like to hear what happened tonight, if you don't mind." When he lowered his voice, Jean sounded downright soothing. It gave me a glimpse of the charisma he possessed to gain the high-ranking position.

Elo noticed it too, judging by the pink that tinted her cheeks. "I was walking home after classes, and the man was just . . . there . . . in the woods." Her voice cracked at the end.

Jean crouched to meet Elo's gaze. "Do you always come home this way?"

"No, I saw the wagon and thought some tea sounded nice. I had some the other day."

"But then you saw the man in the woods?"

"I heard something." Her focus returned to the tea, but I knew she didn't see the drink at all. "It sounded like someone yelling, but muffled. I stepped off the road to look further just as the man fell to the ground. He . . . He wasn't breathing . . ."

Heavy sobs cut off her story. Suzie rubbed Elo's back until her shaking stopped.

"I tried to help him breathe. I put my hands on his chest. But it didn't matter . . . it didn't matter . . ."

She started crying again. Jean sat back on his heels and watched the tears stream down the woman's face. He knew she wouldn't say anything helpful tonight. She needed time to recover and relax.

"Thank you so much for trying to help that man, Elo." Sheriff Jean put a hefty hand on her shoulder. The weight must have distracted her from the tears for a moment. "Remember, you did everything you could. You're a hero for trying, Elo."

Suzie squeezed tighter, and Elo nodded, but the tears continued wetting her face. Jean stood and grabbed Leof's arm to move out of the witness's earshot. I followed. Elo needed some more hot tea to calm her nerves. I'd have Suzie work on that before we left.

"She needs to calm down before we ask anything else." Leof stuck his hands in the loose pockets of his breeches. "I'll have her meet me at the station tomorrow."

Jean nodded. "I think you've got this under control, Marshal. If there isn't anything else, I'm going to head out for the night. There's an assembly in Erline the day after tomorrow, and I need to be there to advocate for some additional funding opportunities. If I miss it, Hallow's Promise will be off the list for new gates until next season."

Jean turned away, but the wheels spinning in Leof's head probably matched the expression on his face.

"Actually, there is something else."

Jean paused and swung back to face Leof. "What is it, Marshal?"

"On the scene, Rae found something. She thinks—"

A little itch developed in my gut as Leof spoke. Whatever made Sheriff Jean dismiss the evidence Pomplo's body may provide spoke for the very little care he would take with my scene. The footprint impressions were the only evidence I had in Valen's disappearance. That itchy part of me didn't want Jean to know about them.

I cut him off. Loudly.

"EVERYONE NEEDS SOME TEA!"

My throat scratched as I belted out the words. People turned to face me—even Elo still clutching her mostly full cup. Suzie's brows shot up.

I cleared my throat. "I mean, sheriff, surely *you* need some nice, relaxing tea before you settle down for the night. I would love to make you a cup of one of my favorites."

Jean scratched his beard. "Now that you mention it, I wouldn't mind a cup of tea. Nothing fancy, of course, but warm sounds pretty damn good."

"Fantastic. Go ahead and wait beside Brew—I mean—the wagon. I want to wrap up with Leof for one moment, and then I'll meet you there."

I didn't wait for the sheriff's reply. I grabbed Leof's arm—oh gosh, I forgot how good he always felt—and dragged him away to the side.

Amber flecks danced in his irises. Uh oh, he was mad at me.

"You didn't let me tell him about the shoeprints." Hm, the words sounded more growly than I would have liked.

"Leof, we can talk about the prints later. I need to know what happens to a body once it's released from an investigation."

He blinked, and the anger dimmed—but didn't fade. "It'll go back to the family. They can arrange whatever religious practices they want after that."

"But Pomplo wasn't from Hallow's Promise. What happens if the family isn't here, or they can't be located?"

He shrugged. "Then the Sheriff's Station assumes responsibility for the body."

"And I work for the Sheriff's Station."

"Yes," he said slowly. "You do."

"Then I assume responsibility for Pomplo's body."

Leof swore. "He's not a puppy, Rae. You can't just call dibs."

"You won't find his family, and you know it." I crossed my arms. "I need to have a closer look at his body and run some tests. If the sheriff won't take him to the morgue, then I will assume responsibility in an official capacity."

"And where are you going to put a dead man? What the hell do you want me to do, throw him on your desk?"

A wicked smile curled my lips.

"Exactly."

Chapter 16

Most offices inside the Sheriff's Station probably had room to fit four people and one dead man.

Mine did not.

"Ouch." Krissa rubbed her chest where my elbow had accidentally poked into her. Although it was the third time she'd leaned forward and blocked my view of the body, so I wasn't sure how 'accidental' my jabs were anymore.

Ilene protested behind her and set one hand on the top of Krissa's head. "Duck your head, woman, I cannot see the intestinal tract."

Krissa blushed at the touch, or maybe the rows of pale organs spreading across my office desk over the vivisected man's abdominal cavity finally got to her.

"Bickering only distracts wandering minds," Alivia murmured from beneath the black mask covering half of her face. Only her vivid, stormy eyes peeked from above the dark fabric.

Alivia was an oddity—even for Hallow's Promise. Her affinity with the dead differed from my own innate abilities. I worked with the magic around life and death. The energy there could be manipulated with a thought or will. Alivia functioned on the physical remains of death. She learned more from cutting someone open than I ever could.

And that gave me the chills.

She plunged her hand beneath the ribcage. A crease caught between her brows as she blindly fished inside. Seconds later, a wet splashing sound released from the body, and Alivia withdrew with Pomplo's heart in her hand.

Krissa turned green. Suzie gagged on the other side of Ilene. The soldier's face remained flat as she watched the carnage on my desk.

That wooden slab would never be the same.

Alivia held the organ toward the light of the flickering lantern. She ran her fingertips along the protrusions and indentations of the muscle.

Alright, fine. My stomach didn't feel great either. When I used to kill and revive people with my power under the directive of the king, I didn't see their insides, and I certainly didn't admire pieces of them in the palm of my hand.

Finally, Alivia set the heart back into the chest. She sighed and turned to our small crowd gathered in the open doorway and spilling into the hall.

"Come here," she said.

I glanced around. Nobody else made eye contact with the mortician. Just me, then? Great. I stepped forward. At least Alivia didn't try to touch me with those soiled gloves.

"Reach inside his mouth."

Every word I knew fell out of my mind.

"Excuse me," I finally spat out.

Alivia blinked. She didn't need her entire face visible to display the utter disgust she held toward my hesitation. "Put your hand inside his mouth."

I glanced around. "Don't you have an extra pair of gloves or anything?"

She rolled her eyes. "Sure, if that's the ridiculous notion holding you back, I do have an extra pair." She thrust a still-bloody hand into her pocket—ew—and pulled out another pair of black leather gloves.

I ground my teeth as I shrugged them on and tried not to think about every dead person the garments had touched.

"Here, I'll hold the jaw." Alivia firmly pulled the man's teeth apart, exposing his gaping mouth.

My stomach turned. Throwing up on the body was not an option. I carefully wriggled my fingers into the space. His tongue pushed against my fingers before I slipped farther beyond the teeth.

I jerked my fingers out. "They don't fit."

"Exactly. This man suffocated on his own tongue. He died from an upper trachea edema, actually, but the other is a simpler way to understand it."

"Ew," Krissa said.

Suzie clutched her throat with both hands. "That's possible? Thank you for the new, greatest fear of my life."

Alivia watched her with a calm demeanor. "You are welcome." She turned to me. I thought I caught a glimpse of laughter in her eyes, but I wasn't sure she could feel anything other than melancholy. "The man was exposed to some kind of allergen. I cannot say exactly what under these . . . conditions. I would like to transport him to my facility for an actual examination."

I pulled the gloves off and thrust them into her arms. "Trust me, I would too, but the sheriff said he can't go to the morgue."

"But he didn't say the man couldn't go onto your office table?" She snorted and turned without waiting for an answer. Wow, did Alivia just make a joke? "I have some supplies to narrow down possible allergens. I will take some blood for testing.

Unless your sheriff has specifically forbidden a vial of blood from entering the morgue?"

Some expression stretched my face. Maybe a grimace, maybe a prequel to the vomit building in the back of my throat.

"He did not say that specifically. Thank you for being willing to do this . . . field autopsy, Alivia."

The mortician gathered the sample vial, then snapped her bag shut and removed the mask from her face. Her sharp nose dipped into a delicate curve at the hollow of her upper lip. Strong cheekbones made her look soft and feminine, but I'd seen a brilliant smile carve across her face right before she thrust her scalpel into a dead body.

"It's always a pleasure to work with you, Rae. I imagine my job would be far less interesting if you didn't handle your cases so thoroughly."

My brow creased. "Um, thanks, I think."

She ducked her head. "My assistant will send the results of the testing. Use caution when cleaning this area since we do not know what he was exposed to."

I glanced between the dead man on my office table and the doorway Alivia slipped through.

"You're not taking him with you?" My voice cracked at the end.

She laughed. "Heavens, no. He's not allowed in the morgue, remember?" Her long robe flicked around her ankles as she chuckled all the way down the hall.

Krissa swallowed—loudly. "What do we do now?"

My brilliant plan hadn't stretched all the way to body disposal. It sort of stopped after Alivia arrived and told me how Pomplo died.

"I guess we have to bury him," I said. "I took responsibility of the body."

"And how do we clean up . . ." Krissa waved her hand at the room in general. "The rest of it?"

Blood and thicker things spread over the wood. I wrinkled my nose.

"I think we have to burn the entire place down."

* * *

In the end, we only burned the desk. I managed to scrub most of the fluid from the floor, and Krissa worked on the walls, even though she complained most of the time. We hesitated when it came time to move Pomplo off the table, but Ilene scooped him up without a word and carried him to the public graveyard near the Sheriff's Station.

The office table quickly followed. While Ilene shoveled dirt into Pomplo's fresh grave, I dismantled the table, wrangled up some kindling, and started a fire.

Krissa, Ilene, Suzie, and I sprawled on the ground before the fire. Bubbles rested on my stomach, his tiny body moving up and down with each breath. I stroked the top of his smooth head and hoped none of his acid drool dropped onto my abdomen. Whiskers rested on the other side of Krissa. His head bobbed up and down whenever anyone shifted, the only indication that he wasn't also snoozing.

"That could have been my brother," Ilene said into the dancing flames.

I let my head tilt back and studied the stars. She'd said what I'd been avoiding all day.

"But it wasn't." Krissa put her hand on Ilene's arm. The

soldier didn't acknowledge the gesture.

"We don't even know if he's still alive."

My heart hurt with each pulse that sent blood through my body. Valen had taught me so much, had believed in me before I believed in myself. He drove me crazy, but he also made me better.

I missed him.

"I found a shoe print at Pomplo's murder scene," I said. "It's the same one from the attackers we fought at Valen's house. I didn't have time to preserve it yesterday, but tomorrow, I'm going back to make a cast."

"What will the cast do?" Ilene asked.

"It will maintain a copy of the print. If we find a suspect, I can use that copy to determine if their shoes match the ones from the scene."

She snorted. "Sounds a little far-fetched."

"Not really. Every shoe is uniquely crafted. Most makers leave some kind of signature on the soles to recognize their work. Pair that with a person's unique gait creating wear on the sole, and it's a great way to identify who was walking around a crime scene."

When Ilene turned to me, a look I hadn't seen before crossed her face. The sadness was still there, but so was something a little warmer.

"Valen said you were special," she said.

My throat tightened. "He talked about me?" And to his own sister.

"He called you Sunshine. I used to think it was just a nickname, but now I think it's something more."

I pressed my lips together. "Like what?" My voice was quiet, weak.

"Intensity, brightness, the sole focus in a blaring blue sky. I think my brother saw all of that in you."

I crossed my hands under my head and looked at the stars again so she wouldn't see me cry. Not that it was bad or because it embarrassed me, but because Ilene turned away when her own tears broke over her cheeks.

Chapter 17

The place where Pomplo died looked the same as any other part of the tree line sandwiching the road. Creatures bristled. Branches blew. Snow melted.

"Tell me again why we're bringing flour to the crime scene?" Suzie huffed as she manipulated the large sack in her hands and tried not to trip on the uneven ground.

"I already told you—it's not flour."

She eyed the bag. "It's a white powder that smells earthy. I don't know what else it could be."

I smiled. Suzie's bag of powdered clay was big and bulky, but the jug of water cutting off the circulation to my fingers was more of a burden to carry out to the scene.

"How far were these prints, anyway?" She continued to grumble, but I ignored her. I'd had a rough night after burying Pomplo. For some reason, the feel of his teeth and cold tongue against my hand kept popping back into my mind. After tossing and turning, I'd given up and moved to the couch with a new recipe book. Bubbles had curled beside me, and soon we were both snoring before the flickering remains of the fire.

"I'm sorry Pomplo's killer couldn't leave evidence in a more convenient location."

She shifted the bag again. "Thank you, Rae, that's all I really wanted to hear."

The diamond of rocks I'd used to mark the evidence remained untouched. I carefully knelt beside the perimeter and removed the closest rock to access the print easier.

Suzie eyed the impression. "It's a little underwhelming, to be honest."

I shrugged. She wasn't wrong. It was barely more than a foot-shaped stamp in the dirt. Little indents marked where each pin secured the thick sole to the bottom of the leather shoe. Visually, it was difficult to decipher the details that identified this shoe specifically. Once the cast was set, they'd be easier to see.

"If you open the bag of powder, there is a sifter inside."

White dust peppered our clothes as she peeled the bag open. The sifter rested on top of the powder, and Suzie pulled it out.

"Now what?"

"Hold the sifter over the impression and I'll dump some powder into it. Then, lightly sprinkle the powder as evenly as possible."

She followed my directions. Her tongue poked between her lips as she concentrated.

"Okay, now that there's a pretty good layer, I'm going to add some water. This part is tricky because if the water is added too quickly, it can disturb the dirt beneath the impression." And this was our only connection to Valen's disappearance. I had one chance to preserve it.

My hand remained steady as I dribbled the water onto the layer of powder. The eager substance soaked in the liquid until it turned into a uniform gray paste.

"More powder. Do it the same way."

Suzie and I traded between layers of powder and trickles of

water. The powdered clay worked beautifully to fill in the tiny spaces along the sides of the shoe print, which hopefully meant it did the same to the pattern on the bottom.

Once wet clay filled the entire impression, I stood and stretched.

"Now what?"

"We have to wait for it to dry completely. Moving the cast early is a great way to destroy it."

Suzie sat back and looked up at me. "What's going on between you and my dad?"

My throat clenched. Heat boiled up my neck into my cheeks. Whatever sound escaped my lips was certainly not words.

"Come on, I know something happened during your last case. Dad's been absentminded ever since."

The ground seemed like the perfect place for this conversation, and if I sat beside Suzie, it would be easier to avoid looking directly at her. I sank into the dirt and let our shoulders touch as we watched the clay dry together.

"I don't know what's happening between me and your dad," I said. "I know undoubtedly that I love him. He saved my life, and I owe him a lot for that."

"But then there's Valen."

I swallowed past the lump in my throat. "Yeah. There's Valen."

"He's saved you, too."

Suzie was more insightful than a young woman her age had any right to be. "Valen hasn't just saved me. He's given me tools and resources to save myself." He reveled in the darkest parts of me. "But I never want to hurt or lie to either of them. If they both want to be with me, I'm going to have to . . . pick one, I guess."

I drew my legs into my chest and wrapped my arms around them. Just shove the knife into my heart and twist it. The thought of living without Valen or Leof made my palms sweaty. They each contributed so much to this new life I loved.

Suzie put her hand on my knee. I studied the contact, where the warmth soaked through my cotton breeches into my skin. A wisp of cinnamon and smoke floated from her, which used to remind me of Leof, but now just meant Suzie.

"If it counts for anything, it doesn't matter to me which one you pick. If you end up with my dad, I'd be happy to have you in my family. But when we rescue Valen and you decide to be with him, I'll always be your friend. You deserve to be happy, Rae."

I grabbed her hand and brought it to my heart. Speaking would unleash a flood of tears I couldn't deal with at the moment. She tightened her grip and the quiet forest noises fluttered around us.

"How's your mom?" I asked when the emotions squeezing my chest eased enough to speak.

Suzie looked up at the sky. "She's fine. Already trying to get me to visit and meet more eligible bachelors. I'll probably have to make a trip over there to stop her from coming here again."

I grimaced. Last time Kara visited Hallow's Promise, she'd ended up being a prime suspect in a murder investigation, and I'd stolen her shawl. We parted on semi-cordial terms only because of Suzie's interference.

"I'm sorry. That sounds awful."

She shrugged. "I think I'm learning to accept my mom for who she is and not who I want her to be. People are weird, you know?"

Branches crunched, and a new voice sliced through our

conversation.

"Yes, they certainly are." My muscles locked at the woman's tone, layered with the depth of a threat. She stepped from the shadows, dressed in all black, including a mesh covering across the entirety of her face. A whip of coiled chain cascaded down from her hip. "And then they're dead."

Chapter 18

I sprang to my feet and shoved Suzie behind me, unsheathing my sword in an easy, practiced motion—which I only had Valen to thank for the hours of repetition of drawing the weapon.

Smoke billowed from the blade. Great, now it decided to do that. When this case was over and Valen was safe, I would make him teach me how to properly Smoke Wield.

The woman pulled the chain whip off her belt and circled us. The rattling sounded foreign among the natural noises. My heart thundered in my chest. Thoughts dimmed to just me, Suzie, and the woman threatening to kill us.

"I should have known you'd return to the scene of your crime," I said. Sometimes gloating an opponent distracted them enough to give me the first strike.

She snorted. "I don't usually have to."

I pressed my lips together. Why would a criminal return to the scene if not to relish in their deeds?

"You left something here, and now you want to hide it," I said. It wasn't a question. I moved slightly to position myself between her and the shoe print impression slowly drying in the spring air. "Well, you're going to have to get past me."

"Us!" Suzie yelled from behind me. I couldn't risk a glance back, but I bet her hands were glowing with whatever golden light she inherited from her mother's side of the family. I'd watched her launch fireballs at shadow creatures once, and certainly never wanted to be on the receiving end.

The woman didn't look at the ground, though. Her gaze shifted upward.

She wasn't here for the shoe print—she probably didn't even know about it. No, she'd left something else at the scene, something we hadn't found yet.

I risked a look this time—I had to. If more evidence remained at the scene, I needed to get to it before she did.

Trees swelled upward from the place where Pomplo's body had rested. The ground was disturbed and uneven from the constables securing the area. Nothing obvious stood out.

The impact of feet on dirt drew my attention back. The woman had taken advantage of my distraction to launch her first strike. That was fine. I was ready.

I lifted my sword into middle-guard, holding the blade diagonally in front of my chest. It was the easiest position to move from if the direction of attack was unknown. Her chain shimmered in the sunlight as it pulled taut with her slash.

My weapon caught hers in the center, but a few of the links wrapped over the top of my sword. The metal whacked into my chest and sent me stumbling backward. My breath caught in the pain.

Ouch. Note to self: don't let that happen again.

This was my first time fighting against any sort of whip weapon. I already hated it. The slim chain was harder to predict than a larger, bladed one.

"Uh oh. Did you get a boo-boo?" she mocked as we circled again. The chain spun in a leisurely circle. "Want another?"

Anger flared hot in my gut. More smoke billowed from the

blade, smothering the sunlight streaming through the canopy.

"You can try."

She crouched down and whipped the chain out in a blur. I jumped over it and struck toward the ground before she retracted the weapon. My blade met metal with an ugly screech, but she tugged the whip back.

A stream of yellow fire flew past my head. I took several steps back while Suzie prepared her next fireball. The attacker yelled as she narrowly dodged the projectile, and it lobbed into the tree behind her. The bark promptly caught fire, and the tree thundered to the ground.

"Well, that's unexpected," the woman said. I couldn't see her face through the thin fabric covering, but her voice sounded adequately surprised.

I didn't have time to compliment Suzie. Her power and aim had increased exponentially since we'd started working together. I'd tell her how proud I was later.

Our opponent studied us for the span of a heartbeat. Whatever she saw made her waver, and she looked up to the same place she'd turned to before. I didn't track her gaze this time.

I stepped forward, and my sword moved into upper guard, an overhead position prepared to strike. I swore the weapon moved itself just a little bit, adjusting the stance right into the center. There wasn't time to ponder my sword slowly gaining sentience—I let the weapon drop toward the woman's hands.

My attacker backed up, a little too slow, and my blade cut into the top of her hand. She cried out as red blood leaked down her fingers onto the metal whip.

Another fireball whirled through the air. She stumbled away, eyes wide, barely avoiding the blast area as it pelted into the ground where she'd just been.

Her chest heaved as she sucked in air. The look in her eyes turned calculating. I saw the thoughts and strategies move through her mind, the same way they would have gone through mine if our roles reversed.

She was outmatched and outnumbered. The stiffening of her body said this rarely happened. We'd caught her off guard.

Which meant her safest option was to flee.

"No!" I yelled as the attacker abandoned the fight and sprinted by us. I shoved my sword into its sheath and followed her, steps behind.

My steps echoed too far behind hers. I'd never catch up.

But she dashed upward into a tree.

I hesitated, unsure of her plan, but she reached into a divot nestled between two branches. A shiny object flashed as she closed her fingers around it.

I reached the trunk of the tree as she dropped out of it. Whatever the woman clenched in her hand became my only focus. The rest of the world narrowed.

She tried to run again, but her climb had given me time to catch up. She managed a step or two, then I flung myself at her. We tumbled to the ground.

Sticks and rocks stabbed me. Sharp cuts stung as my skin split against the forest floor. But it didn't matter. I rolled on top of the attacker and grabbed her wrist in both hands and *squeezed*. She yelled and ground her teeth but didn't open her hand.

I pushed her fist into the dirt. "Give it to me!"

She growled. I forced my fingers beneath hers and pried her hand open, one finger at a time.

The metal flashed in the sunlight. I froze as I glimpsed what she held.

Chains rattled, and a sharp pain exploded inside my head. My vision went dark. The ground smacked into me as I fell backward, releasing the woman from my grip. Burning, icy pain pounded across my face and head.

Distantly, I heard Suzie yell.

"Get away from her!" The zipping sound of her fireballs launched around me. The darkness consumed it all. Only throbbing pain remained.

"Rae!" Suzie's hands touched my shoulder, then lightly grazed my face. A pained sound came from my lips at the contact. "We're safe now. She ran away. Oh, Rae, your face . . ."

It must have been bad because Suzie didn't say anything else. "Come on, I need to get you to my dad. He'll know what to do."

She shifted me into her arms, and the world tilted. I was going to be sick but didn't have the strength to vomit. That woman had hit me across the face and head with her chain whip, and I didn't know what kind of damage that may have inflicted.

"Suzie," I whispered. My tongue felt too big in my mouth.

"It's okay. I'll get you some help." She stepped forward, my much too big body cradled against her side.

Oh, gosh. I might die in the same place as Pomplo. I never saw that coming. But Suzie needed to know what the woman had grabbed.

"A key," I whispered. "She took a key . . ." Breathing hurt. Everything hurt. "For a room . . . at . . . Siren's Sorrow."

There. Now, if I died, Suzie could continue the investigation. Valen would be in good hands.

Then, the world went black.

Chapter 19

Everything hurt less. Not by much, but less.

I groaned as I rolled over. Something soft cushioned my body. Pain concentrated across the left half of my face and head. At least the throbbing ache meant I was still alive.

"Well, look who decided to wake up." Leof's familiar voice and the musty leather scent that was all him told me exactly where I was—inside Leof's house.

I reached for my face, but he caught my wrist. His touch both heated the center of my body and released a rush of comfort.

"I wouldn't touch that, if I were you. We've been putting snow on it, but the swelling is still bad."

I nodded but Leof kept my hand in his. His voice dropped. "We could have lost you."

"Why did I survive?"

He chuckled. "Are you having regrets about our intervention?"

"Of course not." I almost snorted but sucked in a breath as new pain spread beneath my skin. "It was just me and Suzie when everything went black."

"Suzie dragged you to the road, and apparently Brew was already waiting there. She got you into the wagon and looked for a healing potion, but the cupboards were bare. She brewed one all by herself, and it kept you alive long enough to bring you here."

"How bad was the wound?"

Leof shrugged. "I only saw the inside of your head a little bit."

Ew. "She hit me with a chain whip."

"That's what Suzie said." He turned away, but I caught a glimpse of amber in his eyes. I narrowed my gaze and studied the man. His grip on my wrist was a little too tight. A firmness tensed his shoulders.

"You're angry," I whispered.

He looked back at me. Golden light completely consumed his usual brown irises. The muscles twitched beneath his skin. Leof was dangerously close to losing control of his human form. I'd watched him turn into a wolf before, but never when he was so angry.

"Why?"

He shot to his feet. "Why? Why, Rae?"

"I'm fine. Suzie saved me. Nothing happened."

"Nothing?" He shook his head. A vibration tremored through his body. "I watched you tremble on my couch for hours, knowing that my daughter was the only reason you survived. Something could have happened to you and her . . ." His words trailed off, and he sucked in a breath. "I couldn't live without either of you."

I slowly lifted my head. The world only swam slightly, which I took as a good sign.

"You should be proud of Suzie. She did really well."

Leof crouched beside me again. The trembling grew worse. "I am proud of her. But I need to make sure this can never happen again." He reached out and stroked my cheek, so tender despite the barest thread of control he clung to. "Do you know who did this to you?"

"So, you can rip them apart limb from limb?"

"Yes, exactly."

I tried to shake my head, but the dizziness made bile climb up my throat. "I'm sorry, Leof, I don't know who she was. But I intend to find out, and you're welcome to help with the limb tearing."

He grabbed the back of my neck and slowly pulled my head toward his. Our foreheads touched. I closed my eyes and savored the moment of intimacy.

"Never do that to me again," he said.

"I'll try my best."

"Not good enough."

"That's all I have."

He sighed. "I have to run off some of this energy. Promise me you'll be here when I get back."

"I promise." I didn't have many other options, but Leof didn't need to hear that.

He pressed his lips to my forehead and stood. I watched him walk to the back door, shedding his shirt along the way. The way he touched me, and the fine lines of muscles across his back made chills run down my spine. A moment later, the door clicked shut, taking the man and all my confusion with him.

"I hear I have you to thank for my miraculous survival," I said.

Suzie rounded the corner of the hallway, where I'd heard her sneaking around while Leof talked to me. She walked to the couch and perched on the side.

"I accept thanks in the form of financial compensation."

I managed to snort this time with minimal pain. "I'll let you know when I have any of that. But seriously, healing potions are tricky to make. You did a good job."

"Thanks. Why do you think the lady went back for the key?"

"I don't know. Do we have to go back for the shoe print cast?"

"No." A sort of sly smile crossed Suzie's face. "I went back for it once dad was busy taking care of you. Why didn't she try to mess up the print?"

I gave a little shrug. "She might not have known about it, or maybe she didn't care. Very few people understand the type of work we do. Hey, I promised your dad I'd stay here until he gets back, but can you do me a favor?"

"Sure, anything."

"I want to see a mirror."

Her face immediately twisted. "No, you don't."

"Yes, I do. If you don't get me one, then I'll try to find it myself, and I'll probably throw up on your floor."

She sprang to her feet. "Please do not do that. I'll be right back."

It didn't take long for Suzie to return with the mirror. She handed it to me, reflection-side down. "Don't be too alarmed. I'm sure once the swelling goes away, it'll be normal again. The healing potion took care of most of the . . . cracks."

I flipped the mirror upright. *Oof.* My stomach twisted into knots at the face I didn't even recognize. A trail of dark bruising ran across most of the left side of my face. It narrowly missed my eye, grazing along the cheekbone. The coloring spread into a vague chain shape, showing where each link smacked against my skin. Leof must have washed the blood from my hair and face, but a huge knot protruded from the side of my head.

I passed the mirror back. "Thanks, I think."

"You should get some rest." Suzie patted my shoulder.

A wave of dizziness overwhelmed me. I had taken a handful of metal to the side of my head—I guess I deserve to feel a little awful.

"I have so much to do," I whispered. The pain made me feel small, weak. After Valen had once broken into my house in the middle of the night, I'd vowed never to feel that way again. All the effort I'd put into learning sword fighting and self-defense disintegrated at this moment.

Maybe Suzie recognized some of that pain. She scooted beside me and wrapped her arm carefully around my shoulders.

"It's not a weakness to rely on your friends, Rae. That's what we're here for. Tonight, we take care of you. Tomorrow, we will keep searching for Valen."

I turned to rest the good side of my face into the crook of her neck.

"Thanks, Suzie."

Friends—a word I was still getting used to.

* * *

The city wall surrounded the entirety of Hallow's Promise— with the exception of Spirit's Peak, which proved too tall and too wide to entrap entirely. Directly inside the perimeter of the wall, but before most urban areas started, were the Brims. My cottage lived in the West Brim.

A brown envelope rested in front of my door on the front porch. Someone must have dropped it off while I was asleep on Leof's couch last night because I hadn't felt the wards alert me to any intruders on my property.

Looped handwriting scrawled across the top of the envelope:

Your allergy tests.

• *Alivia*

"Do I want to know why the mortician is sending you presents?" Leof leaned against the doorjamb while I struggled with the lock. I grimaced. He didn't exactly know about the illicit autopsy I'd hosted in my office.

"Probably not." The door opened, and the wards lifted, allowing Leof and I to step inside.

The fireplace immediately roared to life. I stopped a mere step beyond the doorway.

"Bubbles!"

White shards littered the floor. If I looked closely, the speckled marrow hugging the outer walls of the bone would be visible. I didn't want to look closely, I wanted the warplog to take his regurgitated bones outside of the house.

Bubbles hopped onto the back of the couch, putting his back to the fireplace. I swore he smiled at me, and his long tongue flicked out. He licked one eyeball, then the other, without shifting his gaze from my face.

I sighed and scooped him up. At least the Oracle was safe inside Brew's cupboard. "What am I going to do with you?"

His beady eyes seemed to widen as he looked at my face. He grunted once, low and deep, which I took as an apology for whatever had messed me up so bad.

I kissed the top of his head. "I'm okay."

"What does the letter from Alivia say?"

"It's the results of Pomplo's blood tests to see what he was allergic to that killed him." I slipped my finger beneath the wax seal, and it released with a satisfying pop.

"Do I want to know how Alivia obtained a sample to test Pomplo for allergies?"

I shrugged. "Probably not."

"The list of things I don't want to know keeps growing."

The clinical summary of Alivia's findings didn't make complete sense to me. I skipped over the words containing more than thirteen letters to the summary near the bottom.

In conclusion, all testing results display the morphology of a folded protein similar to that found in the toxic saliva of the native Erlinian Tick. It is the opinion of this expert that the dosage sustained in the blood was enough to incapacitate without stunting the respiratory system; however, this individual sustained a severe allergic complication resulting in death.

Leof read the note over my shoulder. "Do you understand any of that?"

"Yes." My heart pounded while I read the note again. "It means someone is using toxic ticks to create a paralysis poison. Pomplo was allergic to the ticks, and he died because his throat swelled shut."

"Whoever took Pomplo wasn't trying to kill him?"

I folded the letter and studied the bone shards across the floor. Even though the smile hurt my face, my lips tilted up anyway. If the culprit hadn't been trying to kill Pomplo, that meant Valen could still be alive.

But each delay made that chance less and less likely.

"I need to go to the Siren's Sorrow." I turned to Leof. My

head hurt. My eyes were starting to swell shut. The world spun if I moved too fast. "But I can't do it on my own."

Leof reached out and ran his fingertip along my uninjured cheek. Chills sprinkled down my spine. "I promised to help you find Valen. I'm all yours, Rae, for whatever you need."

I swallowed. "Thank you."

Chapter 20

A hush fell over the Sorrow when Leof and I stepped inside. I wished it was because the thieves of the underground recognized Leof as the town's marshal, but I feared the bruises across my face were the real culprit.

I headed to the bar, giving the rest of the room my back. Their eyes still burned my skin.

Lillie stared at me for a long time. Her gaze shifted to Leof.

"Dear." The bartender grabbed my arm and hauled me halfway across her bar top. "If that man hurt you, I can make sure he's never seen again. You just say the word."

If smiling didn't hurt so badly, I would have let my face light up. "It's okay, Lillie, Leof didn't do this to me. Actually, he stitched everything back together."

Her glare said she didn't quite believe me. "The offer stands . . . if you ever change your mind."

"I appreciate that, I really do. But I'm wondering if I could look over your logbooks for the rooms upstairs?"

"Is this part of the search for Valen?"

"Yes, it is."

She tapped her fingers along the bar, then picked up a food tray from the counter. "I can't officially let you look at the books, dear, but I will be spending several minutes delivering this order to the table in the back." She jerked her chin in that direction. "Be sure to avoid all the logs beneath the other side of the bar while I'm gone."

"Thanks, Lillie."

The woman faded into the crowd, and I circled to the other side of the bar.

"Didn't she just tell you not to do that?" Leof crossed both arms on the wood. His brown eyes sparkled as he watched me.

"What? I'm not doing anything."

I flipped the book open. Neat little rows of names, dates, and payment amounts penciled along straight lines. I recognized some of their names, but others were strangers. None of them jumped out as kidnappers searching for criminals and a severed head.

Leof knew more of the people involved in the underground societies of Hallow's Promise. I flipped the ledger to him. "Do any of these names look weird to you?"

The wolf pressed his lips together but accepted the book. Bending the rules made him itch.

Golden eyes scanned the pages. His brow creased.

"None of the names stand out, but look at this." He pointed to the scrawled name near the bottom of the list. "Dymetri's renting a room here for a whole week."

"So what? Dy is here all the time."

Leof snorted. "Yeah, he's here all the time—selling product and causing trouble. He has a place in East Brim and wouldn't need to rent a room here."

"If he has a house within walking distance, why would he stay here?" I didn't think Dy brought in enough coins to enjoy a leisurely hotel retreat.

"Who knows?"

Lillie returned with her tray as I shoved the book back onto its shelf. "Lillie, I was wondering if you've seen Dymetri lately?"

"I haven't actually, not in a few days."

I tilted my head. "But he's renting a room at the Siren's Sorrow right now?"

"That's odd. I don't remember putting his name down." She reclaimed the book and flipped through the pages. Her finger hesitated on his name before she looked back at us. Her eyes widened, and she leaned closer to lower her voice. "That's not my handwriting. I don't know who put Dy in this logbook."

I had a sinking feeling that Dymetri's sudden appearance in Lillie's book and his seeming disappearance from the Sorrow were connected.

"Well, Dy asked me to drop something off in his room." My voice sounded bright and happy, just in case any interested parties decided to overhear. "Can I borrow the key?"

The bartender didn't hesitate. She slipped the master key from its place on the wall and held it out to me.

"Room 209," she whispered.

* * *

The stairs creaked as we ascended. I'd stayed at the Sorrow once during an early investigation. Valen had inserted himself into my job and ruined a perfectly good stakeout. The room had one bed, which I hadn't been about to share with the mercenary, and we'd both ended up on the floor, staring at each other beneath the bedframe.

I missed him. I missed the icy chill that his anger wrapped around me. I missed his laughter, the way he called me

Sunshine. Each rattling step brought me closer to finding him.

The door to Room 209 didn't look intimidating. It matched the rest of the plain, unpainted pine doors through the hallway.

We paused before the room. Leof pressed his finger against his lips, leaned his head to the door, and closed his eyes. They snapped open seconds later. He held up one finger—there was one person inside.

I nodded in understanding. The marshal pointed to his chest, then to the door. He pointed at me, then to the floor.

I narrowed my eyes. He wanted me to stay in the hallway while he charged whoever was in the room pretending to be Dymetri? Hell, no.

The wolf read my answer in my expression and rolled his eyes. He shrugged, and I pulled my sword. No smoke, of course, because why would it. Leof held up three fingers. He mouthed the numbers as he lowered a digit for each.

Three.

Two.

One.

Leof twisted the knob. The door banged against the wall as it slammed inward. He jumped in first, and I followed his tracks with the blade at middle-guard.

A strange man—that was certainly not Dymetri—stared at us for a heartbeat. He wore mostly black, with a leather coat over the top of his tunic. He had short, blond hair, almost white against his head, and he was tall.

The room consisted of a tiny bed squished in the opposite corner, a window overlooking an alleyway, and one table with a wooden chair near the center of the room—where the man had stood at our entrance.

I sucked in my gut. "We're here for Dymetri. Where is he?"

Blondie blinked. He studied my face, and a wicked smile crossed his lips.

"You're the one sssshe hit, huh?" His gaze burned like acid as he stared at the injuries on my face. "Sssshe'll be happy to hear you ssssurvived. Or, maybe she won't."

White rage stole my vision. He knew the woman who hit me with her chain whip. He knew where Valen was—he had to.

I sprinted across the room. Leof yelled, running at my heels, but his voice faded into the burning rage in my chest. Blondie was involved in Valen's disappearance, and I'd make him be involved in his rescue, too.

Blondie pulled out a cute little knife as I approached. It wouldn't be any match against my blade, which had decided to start smoking a bit. His eyes widened, and I smiled. He'd recognized the smoke, which meant this was the same assailant I'd choked with my Smoke Wielding before. His weariness made my heart sing with joy.

I launched with the sword. He was fast, I'd admit that, but my anger made me better. He dodged the first strike, but couldn't avoid the second one I returned lightning quick. His skin split beneath my blade. A satisfying red liquid oozed onto the hardwood floor.

Blondie retreated. He covered the slash across his arm with his free hand and grimaced. We didn't give him time to recover. Leof launched next, a furred streak that flew by me in wolf form.

As a werewolf, Leof easily reached my hip. Blondie was no match as those clawed paws dug into his shoulders. More blood flew, and the pair rolled onto the ground.

Snarls and yells escaped their flurry as I panted hard. I

couldn't look away from their fight, or I'd miss an opportunity to jump in and stab the guy myself. Of course, I didn't want to stab him too much and risk killing him before finding Valen's location. Just a little stabby stab, that's all I needed.

Leof did a cool roll-chomp, flipping his shaggy body on top of Blondie's. He snapped at the man's face, forcing Blondie to use both hands to keep the wolf's teeth away from his throat. His face twisted. It was a losing battle, and he knew it.

A shadow danced in the hallway. I looked up in time to see another figure dressed in black dart out of the doorway.

The woman—Pomplo's killer.

I hesitated, torn between the man currently at our mercy and the woman fleeing down the hall.

Leof paused, too.

Blondie did not.

The wolf yipped as Blondie's tiny blade sank into the base of his neck. It wouldn't kill the werewolf—they healed from almost anything—but it distracted him enough to give Blondie the upper hand.

The pair rolled again, this time with Leof on the bottom.

Enough. Valen was gone. My face was royally messed up. Leof had been hurt.

My power itched for release. I knew how it would feel to grab the man's life and take it away. Using my magic would bring the king to Hallow's Promise, but that threat felt like it shrunk more day by day. Ilene was already here. Krissa was smitten with her. Leof was disobeying the sheriff to help me find a mercenary. The rebellion was basically at my doorstep already.

But I knew I couldn't do it. Fear had locked away that option in my mind. I couldn't even uncover it now.

I also didn't need it.

I crashed the hilt of my sword into the back of Blondie's head. The man yelled out, and Leof scooted from beneath him. When Blondie turned to me, his face lit with murderous intention. I smiled.

It didn't hurt this time.

My sword crashed to the floor. I fisted my fingers exactly how Valen taught me and let my fist slam into Blondie's face. His lip split. His head snapped back. He didn't have time to swing at me before my other fist greeted his cheek.

The anger was uncontainable. It fed me, made me strong. I let it sing from my soul as I punched Blondie in the face again and again, until blood spewed from his mouth and nose. He slumped to the ground. I delivered one more hit to make sure he stayed there.

I leaned over and sucked in deep breaths. Punching someone for real, and not just in a sparring circle, was more exhausting than practicing. My fingers trembled and ached. Blood—mine and his—covered my fingers.

But wow—I felt amazing. Undefeatable.

"Where. Is. Dymetri?" The words were sharp. They grew louder. "Where. DID. YOU. TAKE. VALEN!" The entire inn probably heard me.

Blondie *laughed*. "Don't worry. The Bosssss is taking good care of them. Though, maybe not for long, ssssince I think we found what we've been looking for."

I lifted my arm to punch him again, but a pained noise stilled my hand. Leof, back in human form, curled in the corner and clutched his throat.

"Which issss it, little necromancer?" The world froze. I turned back to the man below me. Blood covered his face and stained his teeth red. "Me or your friend?"

I didn't have time to dwell on how he knew what—who—I was. "The knife was poisoned."

"Yessss. You are a sssssmart one, huh?"

"It's not a lethal poison." But Pomplo had died. Did I want to risk Leof's life?

"Maybe, maybe not."

A frustrated yell left my lips. I had to help Leof. He was more important than Blondie right now, even if it hurt to leave the man on the floor and walk to the werewolf.

Leof's eyes flickered rapidly. He was naked, which usually I would have appreciated, but it only added to the helplessness of his shaking body on the floor.

A crunchy sound followed by a loud crash came from the other side of the room. Blondie was gone, leaving a broken window and shattered glass in his wake. I jumped to the sash, knowing it was far too late for me to do anything.

Two shadows moved on the cobbled street below. The woman slung an arm over Blondie's shoulders to help him walk. It made me a little happier knowing I'd injured him that badly.

I sighed and pulled the comforter off the bed. Maybe a gross kidnapper had slept with it, but I knew defending a shred of Leof's dignity was most important tonight. The cover trailed behind as I locked the door, then flung the fabric over the wolf's shaking form.

The ground was hard as I sank beside him. There was a bed in this room, but it would be impossible for me to pull Leof all the way there and onto the mattress. My hands were a mess from hitting Blondie, and my head hurt more than ever.

But I refused to leave my friend frightened and alone on the floor.

I tucked the blanket tight around Leof. He whined, a mix of man and wolf. I stroked his hair away from his face.

"I know you're scared." I leaned down and pressed my forehead against his cheek. His cinnamon smoke smell rubbed onto me. "It's only a paralyzing toxin. You're going to be okay. It won't last forever."

I nestled into the crook of Leof's body and wrapped my arm around him. He sucked in a breath of my scent, but continued shaking as he tried to fight the toxins. He was a healthy werewolf, they wouldn't last long.

I repeated my mantra to both of us. *You're going to be okay. It won't last forever.* Eventually, Leof stopped shaking. He couldn't speak, so I spoke for both of us. I told him how well Suzie did with her lessons. How Krissa had a new crush—though I didn't specify who. And how much he meant to me as one of my best friends.

I don't know who fell asleep first. At some point, I rolled my back against Leof's stomach, and his arm moved just enough to wrap around me and pull me closer.

You're going to be okay. I thought to myself, half enveloped in a dream. *It won't last forever.*

Chapter 21

The distilling still resembled an archaic torture device. One large container held water beneath a mesh pan, which funneled steam through a contraption of small copper pipes. The pipes ended in a smaller container, where the precious oil and water gathered prior to final separation.

Usually I hated distilling oils, but it was a fantastic way to channel my anger into a useful task.

The bushels of lavender released a lovely, springtime scent through Brew's interior. I'd half rolled the sash up, not enough to falsely advertise that we were open, but plenty of space to allow the sunshine and fresh air to mingle with the lavender stalks.

Coals burned in the inset fireplace, low enough to keep the water in the bottom of the still boiling, but not hot enough to make all of us sweat. The liquid bubbled quietly beside me while I packed the lavender into the mesh screen of the still.

The stalks gave a satisfying crunch as I smashed them harder into the mesh. I added another handful, gleeful as I shoved the violet flowers together despite their protests.

"So, you found one of the kidnappers?" Krissa asked.

"Yep."

"And you almost incapacitated him?" Ilene chipped in. The

woman still wore that ridiculous armor, which rattled every time she moved, and made Bubbles glare out of his cupboard as his nap was disturbed.

"Uh, huh."

"But then he ran away?" Krissa's brows rose—like this was the part of the story she didn't understand.

"He jumped through a window."

"So, instead, you slept with the werewolf?"

My cheeks burned at Krissa's question. She asked so flatly and casually, as if it meant nothing at all.

"I didn't *sleep* with Leof. We both slept next to each other. Independently."

"But he was naked?"

I choked. "He had changed from his wolf shape back to his normal shape. He's magic—his clothes aren't. He was naked, but not by choice."

"But you shared a blanket," Krissa said.

Yes, when I'd woken the next morning, part of the blanket had drifted over me. And part of me may have been pressed against part of Leof—and his part may have been pretty happy about that. And I *may* have pretended not to notice anything. I casually tossed him his half-shredded breeches and sprinted out of the room as quickly as possible.

Krissa wiggled her eyebrows. "How impressive is his . . . weapon?"

The blush climbed up my cheeks. Fire, I was on fire.

"Shut up."

"No," Ilene said. "She makes a good point. A well-endowed man is naturally considered attractive to most women. Did he impress you?"

"I. Am. Not. Talking. About. This." I ground my teeth. "My

priority is finding Valen, not discussing the size of men's . . . weapons."

"Perhaps you'd benefit in comparing their levels of attractiveness."

Oh, my . . . I refused to have this conversation with Valen's *sister*. "I'm sure Valen's . . . weapon is very attractive." My face hurt from the bruising and the burning. "The point of the story wasn't to discuss Leof. It was to tell you the progress we've made in Valen's case—which is almost none."

"And Dymetri is missing, too."

"What do we do now?"

I smashed more lavender into the screen. "Leof got a good sample of the male kidnapper's scent, so he'll be able to make a scent map. But that doesn't do us any good if we don't have a suspect for comparison."

Ilene adjusted her armor. "Can't you use a spell to track the man now that you have his scent?"

"No, it doesn't work like that. I can track inanimate objects, and they have to be marked with a specific symbol."

She huffed.

No more blooms could possibly fit inside the strainer. I settled the mesh screen above the boiling water. Steam rose and immediately mingled with the stalks, sending even stronger lavender vibes through the wagon. Lavender was supposed to instill calmness and relaxation. It didn't feel like it was working.

Ilene eyed the contraption as I fit the elongated top and its winding pipes over the steaming flowers. "That looks impractical."

"It sort of is. I usually distill my oils at home, on my kitchen table." Today, I wanted to be close to Brew. The wagon vibrated as though it knew my very thoughts. Maybe it did. I guess I didn't really know what a magic wagon could do.

I checked on the smaller container that would gather the lavender steam as it condensed against the top of the still. The coveted oils would be released with the water and—once it cooled—I'd be able to separate the layers. A few droplets already gathered at the valve.

Ilene flinched when I turned back toward her. "Once I find the culprit that marked your face, I will relieve their head from their body."

"You'll have to get in line." I gently prodded the outline of the bruise on my face. At least my eye hadn't swollen shut. Small victories were all I had right now.

The drops of mixed lavender water and oil oozed into the glass at the end of the still. I felt more like the stalks on the screen than the precious components embedded in the liquid. A fire slowly cooked me from the outside and stripped away all the things I held precious.

I still didn't have Valen. I didn't even know where to look next.

A knock sounded against the window. Bubbles opened one eye long enough to groan, and Whiskers barely shuffled his head free from where it tucked against the warplog.

I froze, my heart hammering. Enough had happened lately that I wouldn't be surprised if someone greeted me sword-first at the sash.

But when I rolled the wood up, a familiar, delicate face and sharp nose greeted me with a smile.

"Elo," I said, a little surprised. I knew the moment Elo noticed the wounds on my face. Instead of asking, she looked pointedly away with a frown.

Krissa stood on her tiptoes to look over my shoulder. "Who's Elo?"

"She's . . . a customer." That was easier than explaining she was also a witness to a murder. "Elo, this is Krissa—one of my friends."

Krissa held her hand through the opening. "Her *best* friend."

Elo chuckled and returned the handshake. "It's lovely to meet you, Krissa-Rae's-Best-Friend."

"How can I help you?" I asked.

"I'm on my way home from the Sheriff's Station, actually. Marshal Leof had some more questions about the . . . incident I saw. He mentioned he had another appointment, though, so I couldn't stay long. I saw the wagon on my way home and thought I'd see if you're selling drinks today."

"I'm sorry, but today's just a restocking day. I've got some lavender oil processing right now. It'll make a delicious tea once . . ." Once I felt ready to start selling again. Once Valen was safe. "We open again."

"Oh, I see." She turned away, but not before her eyes turned misty. My throat clenched. Tea wasn't the only reason Elo had approached Brew.

"Elo, wait," I said softly.

Armor creaked as Ilene stretched to look over me as well. "Is the smaller woman crying?"

I barely avoided smacking my palm against my forehead. Clearly, Elo was upset about something, and the amount of emotional support inside the wagon was lower than usual.

"Wait right there, I'm going out. Excuse me." I edged around the giant consuming most of Brew's interior, angling toward the door in the back.

Brew threw the door open before I touched the lock. I patted the doorframe in gratitude and circled around to Elo.

"I'm sorry." She wiped her eyes roughly with her fingertips, and her breath rattled as she spoke. "I didn't mean for you to see me like this. I've just been so upset."

"What's wrong, Elo?" I didn't know her well enough to embrace her, so I settled for grabbing her hand. "You can tell me if you'd like."

Her eyes turned distant. "I can't stop seeing him."

"Who?" Was someone threatening her?

"That man! The man who died on the side of the road like an unwanted animal. His eyes were so . . . empty. He felt all wrong." She studied her palms as if Pomplo's blood still stained them. "Every time I close my eyes, the memory of his face appears. How can you live like this? How can you see something like that and sell tea the next day?"

Ah, I should have known someone so unfamiliar with death would react this way. Leof would have more resources, but I could only speak from my heart.

"Because of practice, Elo." I rubbed my thumb against the back of her hand in a small comfort. "The first time I saw a dead body, I couldn't sleep for a week. The second time was easier. But it's never *easy*. It never feels right."

"Then why do you keep going back?"

I didn't know how to explain the feeling. When I held a deceased person, I was one of the last to do so on this earth. It's an honor to complete the one deed they are unable to accomplish—helping them find justice. Elo didn't get any of that closure. She only saw the worst parts.

"When I go to a scene, especially a murder, there's a part of me that never leaves it. I chip off a piece of myself knowing that I can't be whole again. But neither can that victim. Neither can their families. I leave that part there because I take something even better with me—respect, honor, and the knowledge that I did something good."

Elo's eyes flashed. My brow creased. The expression faded before I'd deciphered it. "What do you do when there's nothing left of you?"

I laughed—dry and humorless. "I don't know yet, but I do know that hasn't happened to you. Part of you will stay with Pomplo in that forest. The rest of you will move forward, getting better day by day."

"No," she whispered. "I'm not sure there's much left to move forward." Elo straightened and shook her head. She stared at our hands touching for a moment, then carefully drew her fingers from mine. When she looked at me, she smiled. "Thank you, Rae. That was very helpful."

"Um, you're welcome." It hadn't felt like I'd helped much. Hopefully she'd caught the sincerity in my words. "Please come back if you ever want to talk again. Next time, I'll have a delicious lavender tea just for you."

"Thanks, I'd like that."

Krissa and I waved as Elo strolled away. Once she went around the curved bend and carefully crossed the road to the other side, Krissa leaned into me.

"She's weird."

I couldn't disagree. That flicker in her eyes had been . . . weird.

Hm, I hadn't been on this side of the wagon in a while. The Brew-Tea-Ful sign was a little crooked. I stepped toward it.

"You didn't tell me the sign was crooked." I gently chastised the wagon, which bounced in a careless, *you're not the boss of me,* attitude. The sign straightened easily. I wished my life would do the same.

My step back toward the wagon's door crossed over Elo's prints in the dirt. My mind caught on the image enough to make me pause. For a moment, my eyes and brain struggled to form a coherent thought.

The footprints . . . appeared familiar.

My heart sped up. A lump caught in my throat.

"Look!" I pulled Krissa's arm. She followed my line of sight, and her brow creased. "I need the shoe print cast inside Brew's upper cupboard."

"You don't need the cast. I can tell from here—that's the same shoe as the person who killed Pomplo."

Damn, she was right.

Elo was Pomplo's killer—and Valen's kidnapper.

Chapter 22

I compared the casts anyway. Brew vibrated while I studied the impression Suzie and I had made at Pomplo's murder scene to the new cast of Elo's shoes in the mud. The prints outside of Valen's house were only preserved in my mind, but I had no doubts.

They were all the same.

"So, Elo kidnapped Valen." Krissa paced the handful of steps it took to cross from each side of the wagon. "Why?"

I hung my head over the casts. I wanted to cry. Finally, a real lead, something that might take me to Valen.

"I don't know, but it's on the top of my list to ask."

"It may be difficult, asking her when I've removed her head." Ilene stormed forward, her sword half unsheathed. Krissa caught her arm. It wasn't the first attempt she'd made to follow Elo since my footprint discovery less than an hour ago.

Krissa held her in place—only because Ilene allowed her to—while I spoke. "If you kill Elo, our only lead toward Valen's location will be gone. It will make her accomplice more on edge, and we might lose the trail—again."

She turned to me. "You are supposed to find my brother. So far, you've created two clay footprints and let one of his kidnappers escape. Maybe it's time to try things *my* way."

I spun away from her. The words on the tip of my tongue would not deescalate the situation, but I also didn't want her to see the hurt on my face. Of course, she had far more right to be upset about the lack of progress than I did. Valen was her family, they shared the same blood.

But didn't friendship count for anything?

"Rae is doing everything she can." Krissa's voice broke through the pain clamping my chest tight. "She cares about your brother. You can trust her."

Silence rang for a few seconds.

Ilene sighed. "I apologize. My frustration is not toward you."

I looked back at her. She'd ducked her head, and her blonde braid tumbled down one shoulder. It was a glorious sight, to see a woman as beautiful and proud as Ilene bow her head to someone like me.

"I made you a promise on the first day you came here, Ilene. I promised to find Valen, and I will keep it. But I'm going to need your help."

Golden light flashed in her eyes. "Anything."

"Do you have any allergies?"

Her perfect brows creased, and her mouth opened, but Krissa popped in before Ilene spoke.

"No. Absolutely *not.*"

I blinked. "It's the only way to find exactly where these people are taking their prisoners. Now that we know who's doing this, we can set up a trap."

But Krissa shook her head, sending a rainbow shower of ribbons around. "You are not using Ilene as bait."

The soldier's gaze darted between us. "What is this . . . bait?"

"She wants you to get taken by these kidnappers so she can use you for a tracking spell. But it's statistically unlikely to succeed."

"Is it, or are you afraid something will happen to your girlfriend?"

Krissa's cheeks turned pink, and she made a choking noise. I continued.

"Leof has agreed to help with the investigation. Together, we can make sure Ilene remains as safe as possible."

But Ilene's attention had slipped from me. "Girlfriend?" she asked, softly. "Explain that."

My friend ducked her head, apparently having no intention of answering Ilene's request.

I sighed. "A girlfriend is a woman you care about more than just a friend."

"Like a sister?"

"Ew, no. It's someone you want to have a relationship with. You know, kissing, holding hands, stuff like that."

She turned to Krissa. "And you wish to do those things . . . with me?"

Krissa still didn't answer.

Ilene stepped closer to the other woman and tucked her fingers beneath her chin. Krissa lifted her head and stared into Ilene's crystal eyes.

"I must find my brother," the soldier said, in a voice softer than I'd ever heard before. "But before I return to the warfront, I'd like to talk about this term . . . girlfriend."

A few more unintelligible sounds escaped Krissa's lips, ending with the word, "Okay."

Ilene turned back to me. "Tell me your plan, necromancer."

I flinched. "Don't call me that. But Krissa is mostly correct. Elo visited Brew before finding Pomplo's body, and I'd guess she scoped out all her targets before attacking them. Pomplo's death was an unfortunate accident, but it also gave Elo the opportunity to play the innocent bystander role."

"You were probably her next target, then." Apparently, Krissa had found her voice.

"Yes, and I would offer to be the bait." My hands clenched. I would like nothing more than to face Valen's kidnappers myself. "But I'm the only one who can do the tracking spell."

"Why can't I be the bait?" Krissa crossed her arms.

"For the same reason Leof can't do it. You're way too squeaky clean."

"I am not. I can get my hands dirty."

"Name one time you've gotten your hands dirty."

Her mouth opened and closed. "I dumped that water pitcher on Kara's head."

"That is not dirty. In fact, that actually made her cleaner. You'd be awful bait, Krissa. But offering them the leader of the rebel army . . ." I couldn't imagine someone with a greater threat to Hallow's Promise. "Everyone would know she couldn't stick around long. They'd have to abandon their plans to take me, and capture Ilene as quickly as possible.

"And you'd be able to track her successfully?"

"I promise to do everything to the best of my ability to keep Ilene safe."

The soldier snorted, which was honestly the proper response. "I will also keep myself safe. You don't have to worry about me . . . girlfriend."

"I . . . that's not how you use that word. You know what, never mind. We need to talk to Leof. He's better at covert operations than I am."

Hopefully, he wouldn't freak out too much when I walked the Phoenix Queen through the Sheriff's Station and directly into his office.

Chapter 23

Main Street at night was beautiful. Glowing lanterns flicked golden light along the streets. Happy voices floated along the gentle breeze. A thick scent of fresh bread and ale oozed from every door that opened and closed while people milled about. Tourists began to fill the inns as the season promised summertime soon.

In contrast, the Siren's Sorrow looked even more eerie. The people shuffling through its doors wore dark cloaks with the hoods concealing their faces. The ale smelled stronger and the bread stale. Even the lanterns glowed with an amber hue rather than the soft golden light of the others.

"Are you ready?" I asked Ilene, who crouched at my side, hidden among the overgrown bushes toward the rear of the Sorrow.

I hadn't thought the woman could be more beautiful. Then, she removed her armor to look less threatening to our targets. The metal slabs concealed a body honed to perfection, with lines of muscles along her arms that slivered into a tight waist and long legs. She'd tossed that blonde hair into a cascade of curls down her back. One sword—there'd been five concealed in her armor previously—remained around her waist to maintain appearances. The Phoenix Queen wouldn't go anywhere unarmed.

Krissa was drooling. Honesty, I probably was, too. Ilene was gorgeous—it was unfair to the guests inside. She would break their hearts.

"Are you sure you want to do this?" I asked for the twelfth time tonight.

She just looked down her button nose at me.

"Okay." I guess that meant yes. "Leof is already waiting inside, just in case anything unexpected happens. Do you remember the plan?"

"Are you insulting my intelligence? I've organized and led dozens of strategic, wartime maneuvers that put my life on the line. This is not a difficult plan."

"Great. So . . . you're going to go inside and . . . ?"

She sighed. Apparently, all those wartime maneuvers hadn't involved a stubborn necromancer. "I will whisper loudly to the bartender that I am the rebellion leader here to gather intelligence on the enemy. I will give her the rebellion coin, and she 'accidentally' loudly relays my identity to the bar folk."

The rebellion coin didn't exist until earlier tonight. I'd forced Leof to scratch a symbol into the side of a blank coin with his werewolf-claws. I had a twin of the engraving, which I would use for the tracking spell once the kidnappers took Ilene.

"Which should get Elo and her pal over here as quickly as possible. I think you've got it. Be safe, Ilene."

But Ilene didn't head toward the doors of the Siren's Sorrow.

She wrapped her arms around Krissa, pulled Krissa close, and pressed her lips to Krissa's mouth.

My eyes widened, and so did Krissa's around Ilene's shoulder. A heartbeat passed, and Krissa closed her eyes, a little sigh falling from her lips.

It didn't want to watch them kiss, but it felt sort of rude to look away. I compromised by plucking grass beneath my feet until Ilene pulled back.

She tucked a strand of hair back into one of Krissa's rainbow braids. "I will be back for you. I promise."

"I . . . um . . . thank you," Krissa stammered.

Then Ilene melted into the shadows, not as seamlessly as Valen did, but enough that when she stepped onto the walk toward the Sorrow, nobody on the streets glanced her way.

I nudged Krissa with my elbow. "Girlfriend," I said.

She touched her lips, like she wasn't sure what had just happened. "Yeah, maybe. I guess."

A light flickered as Ilene pulled the door open. The glow consumed her figure, leaving us to wait in the darkness.

* * *

A commotion woke Krissa and me a couple hours before sunrise. We'd fallen asleep leaning against each other, taking turns watching the door to the Siren until neither of us kept our eyes open. The stressful week was certainly catching up.

Yells and the striking sound of metal on metal jarred me upright. I peered over the bushes, Krissa at my side doing the same thing. Figures danced in the shadows. Soft silver flickers of swords flashed.

"They're fighting her," Krissa whispered.

She was right. Elo's frame looked painfully familiar now as she danced around Ilene's blows with her chain whip. The other man held a sharpened stake dagger, which delivered quick, accurate motions that Ilene barely dodged.

The two assailants were skilled fighters, undoubtedly, but the careful lines in Ilene's body showed where she held back. Some of her strikes fell too slowly, giving the pair ample opportunity to gain ground against her. If they'd attacked Ilene when she wasn't purposely throwing the fight, she could kill them both.

Elo landed a quick slash against Ilene's side. Krissa sucked in a gasp.

"Shhh, she's okay." But the fight hurt me, too. Ilene had wiggled onto the very short list of people I called friends. "She's supposed to be taken, and I have the coin to track her. It'll be okay, Krissa."

My friend nodded, but remained intently focused on the scene across the lawn.

The man flicked his pointy blade into the edge of Ilene's wrist. She gave them a proper shout, a mix of acting and true anger, and let him have a blow to the side of the head with her hilt. He staggered back. Hopefully, the paralysis toxin would kick in before Ilene accidentally beat them to a pulp.

The trio exchanged a few more blows, but I saw the moment the toxin started working. Ilene shook her head like her vision was blurry, still managing to complete several blocks. Elo landed another strike along her shoulder.

"She's slowing down," Krissa whispered.

"Yes."

Each of Ilene's motions turned jerked, less graceful. Her sword sagged into the dirt, and she heaved it harder with each swing. Elo and the man dodged easily now. They fluttered around her, letting her own increasing heartbeat spread the toxin for them. Finally, Ilene's arms sagged, and she fell to one knee.

The two approached carefully. The sword fell from Ilene's

fingers moments before the woman curled up and toppled to the side.

"It hurts." Krissa ducked down, but seemed unable to tear her gaze from the fight. "Seeing her like that."

I understood what she meant. The Valen-sized hole in my heart recognized that same feeling of loss.

But I knew we would get them back.

The man revealed a coil of rope from a satchel along his back. The pair wrapped loops around Ilene's ankles and pulled her toward the darkened wood. Before we could have followed them, the three disappeared, eaten by the darkness.

Krissa sat on her heels. I wrapped my arm around her shoulder and pulled her close. We sat in the quiet together, thinking about the ones we'd lost.

Temporarily. I reassured myself.

"Ladies." Leof stepped from the shadows. He must have left the Sorrow while watching Ilene's abduction distracted me. "I think Rae has some cider to make."

Chapter 24

The cider tasted just as good as last time. I didn't add any alcohol, although it probably would have eased my tattered nerves. Instead, I let the magic within the ingredients warm me from the inside out as I downed my glass and studied the little golden coin perched at the top of the Hallow's Promise map.

A familiar buzz of magic swept through me. The heat of my necromancy mixed with the eagerness to find Valen. I reigned it in. Having the king of Erline appear at my doorstep would make rescuing Valen a lot more difficult.

But the common magic was safe to use. I uncoiled it from the center of my soul. It wrapped around the map, the wagon, blended into the powerful cider potion I'd brewed over the last hour. Brew sent a wind through the wagon's interior that muffled the candles and dimmed the flames of the oven.

I cradled the pot of cider in both hands. My magic bled into the potion as it swirled, activating the magic of the individual components. The apples were generations removed from the apple of Eden. A lesser-known priestess blessed this water. I'd even grown the cinnamon myself, which had to count for something since I'd accidentally made a magic wagon and a magic sword.

The power filled the concoction. It hummed in my soul and along my skin. Brew buzzed against my feet.

Once the potion heated in my hands, I plucked the coin from the map and tossed it into the liquid. Little waves swallowed the piece whole, and the temperature rose quickly.

My magic sang. I'd once commanded life and death. This was a pale comparison, but one I relished in.

The power reached a peak, and I dumped the entire pot onto the map. I lingered with my eyes closed, envisioning the magic soaking into each tiny drop, how the molecules folded together, guided by my power, to find Ilene's symbol on the map.

Krissa gasped. Leof groaned. It must have worked.

I opened my eyes. Brew had lit the candles again, affording a gentle glow to see the results of the spell.

Liquid gathered across the parchment, except one clear area.

I squinted. "That can't be right."

"Has this spell ever been wrong?" Leof asked.

"No . . ."

"Then it's probably right." He leaned away from the counter, as though the entire prospect disgusted him. I didn't completely disagree.

"Why would Ilene be at the Sheriff's Station?" Krissa asked.

Leof growled. "I don't know."

"Have you seen anything suspicious while you're there? Like, I don't know, people being dragged around by their feet?"

"No." But he rubbed his hand along his chin.

"You're thinking about something," I said. "You only do that when you have an idea."

He froze and dropped his hand. "I was thinking about the old prison. The one that got boarded up when someone's Nightingale trashed the whole place."

"Whiskers was not responsible for his actions at that time." Krissa jerked her chin up. "Since he's been granted autonomy over his powers, he has not destroyed a single prison cell."

"Yeah, yeah." Leof waved her words away. "But the old entrance was boarded up because the staircase was unstable. The contractors created a temporary doorway at the backside of the building to access the interior for repairs. They've been on hold for a few months now since River's Edge had all that flooding and every contractor is working over there."

River's Edge was Hallow's Promise's neighboring village that shared the other side of Spirit's Peak. They'd gotten hit with more mountain runoff after a series of heavy rains wiped out a couple of impoverished neighborhoods.

"Has anyone gone down there since the contractors left?"

Leof shook his head. I bit my lip. It would be the perfect place to stash kidnapping victims. It would also require someone with inside knowledge about the Sheriff's Station to know that the old prison cells were unsupervised.

"Don't you think anyone would hear multiple prisoners yelling for help down there?" Krissa asked.

"No, it's enchanted with silencing spells. They must have remained intact after Whiskers' incident."

"Again, he was being coerced."

"Again, he destroyed an entire level of a building."

I jumped into their conversation before it turned into a fight. "The point is, we have clear evidence that Ilene was taken to the Sheriff's Station. We need a plan to infiltrate it and get all the victims out." Including Valen, if he was still alive.

Please be alive.

"Wow, Rae actually wants to make a plan?" Leof crossed his arms and chuckled. "That's how you know things are bad."

"Well, *plan* is a strong word. More of an outline."

"Of course."

"Are you coming or not?"

"You know I'll be right behind you, no matter how crazy your *outline* is."

Leof offered me his hand. I studied his fingers and the way he held them toward me so effortlessly. I'd once watched him bleed all over his couch after a Provider injured him and threatened Suzie. He knew I was a dangerous friend to have, but he chose me anyway.

I put my fingers in his and he led me out of the wagon.

* * *

Luckily, the Sheriff's Station wasn't very far from the Siren's Sorrow. The station hugged the east side of Main Street, far enough from the attractions that confused tourists didn't accidentally end up inside.

The back of the Sheriff's Station was surprisingly different from the front. The whitewashed stone was replaced with exposed bricks that sheltered crawling ivy from the wood line. Faded grass brushed against the edge of the exterior wall. Soon, it would be warm enough for the stalks to settle higher.

Calling the new entryway into the prison cells a *door* was being polite. Most of the level remained underground, so the contractors dug half of a tunnel against the wall, punched a hole out, and plastered a chunk of warped wood against the opening. It did have hinges, so I guess it was technically a door, but trash was a better description.

"You definitely have mice in there. That slab isn't keeping

anything out." Krissa wrinkled her nose.

Leof's brow creased. "You definitely have mice, too. Everyone has mice."

"Yeah, but my mice have names, so they're allowed to be in my house. I don't think these are the kind of mice with names."

I wasn't about to volunteer to name a prison mouse.

It felt a little silly watching the door as the first rays of sunshine crept along the horizon. We'd found a relatively invisible space between a cluster of shrubs and two thick tree trunks, but if Elo and Blondie decided to venture into the woods, they'd see us fairly quickly.

"I'm thinking that if anyone is inside and they've been awake all night, they're going to want to come out and sleep in their own beds. Nobody wants to sleep with all the mice that are probably inside there."

I flinched at Krissa's words. Valen had been missing for over two weeks. If he was inside the prison, he'd definitely been sleeping with the mice. And honestly, I'd prefer that to some of the other options.

Cold seeped through my clothes. The snow faded away day by day, but the hours before the sun rose remained below freezing. Waves of adrenaline coursing through my body didn't help either. I couldn't stop my fingers from shaking. I ached to slam the door open, draw my sword, and slaughter anyone between me and Valen.

Leof eyed us. "You guys didn't bring the warplog or the Nightingale."

"Of course not. They could get hurt."

He rolled his eyes *so* hard. "Yes, gods forbid you bring the two most formidable creatures on the earth, lest they might get hurt." He glanced at me. "Bubbles could eat either one of those perps with a single bite."

I shrugged. "He was taking a nap. Didn't want to wake him."

"He's *always* taking a nap."

Leof had a point, of course. But I was secretly with Krissa on this. I'd already lost Valen. I couldn't lose Bubbles.

The werewolf might have had more to say, but the hinges on the wooden slab groaned as someone pushed the door open.

"I can't believe you haven't heard that terrible noise before," Krissa whispered.

Elo and Blondie stepped out of the weird trench and climbed up the dirt onto flat ground. They pulled off the mesh face coverings once the slab had returned to its intended position and stuffed them into twin satchels around their shoulders.

They angled toward our little hideout, and the three of us ducked. My heart thundered, but I sort of hoped they'd venture this way. Now that I knew where Valen likely was, I had a sharp sword eager to taste their blood.

But they veered away, toward the road, and their steps echoed on the cobblestones.

Leof popped up and scanned the area. He gestured to Krissa and me that it was clear.

"Alright, Rae, what's next on your *outline?*"

I cracked my knuckles and stretched my neck. This was the easiest part of the plan, the piece I'd been most looking forward to.

"Now we go inside."

And find Valen.

Chapter 25

I was pretty sure the prison hadn't previously looked like this. I'd only spent a brief time there when Krissa was unfairly held for a crime she didn't commit, but I vaguely remembered plain walls, minimal torches, and an overall *sad* vibe.

Whatever changes had occurred since my last visit, the words *evil* and *abhorrent* came to mind.

Trudging through the awkward tunnel and prying the mangled wooden slab open was bad enough. Mud clung to my breeches, which were already stained from rolling around on the ground throughout the night. The hinges screeched just as badly after Leof slashed the lock off with his werewolf claws. He hadn't regained his human hand—just in case he needed claws for a fight.

I'd expected the door to open into the wreckage that remained after Whiskers destroyed the place, including a giant crack across the floor. But the opening spilled us into a pitch-black room, thick with the scent of fresh paint. Rows of cages—far too small to be called cells—lined the wall against the back. The far corner held a small kitchen stocked with preserved foods. A pair of chairs perched around a table, and a deck of cards flopped across the surface. It smelled like piss, and worse.

Figures shifted away from the light as Leof lit a torch.

Whatever trauma they'd been exposed to had taught them light was bad.

Krissa pressed her hand against her mouth. Tears bubbled along the edges of her eyes. I wanted to embrace her, but needed both hands free in case of any unexpected surprises.

The marshal stepped closer to one cage. The poor man inside turned briefly, illuminating his face for a heartbeat.

"Estello?" Leof knelt beside the cage. Nothing more than a whimper came from the man.

"Let me guess, petty criminal?" I asked softly. More of the prisoners jerked at the sounds of our voices.

"A known thief and other small crimes. Mostly tries to pawn stolen goods at the market, and the merchants turn him in."

Selling stolen wares was a good way to lose your booth at the market.

The place, though horrific, was well structured and organized. Someone obviously thought out the cage placements, the room for essentials like food and water, and the drain in the middle allowed for quick and easy cleaning—though for what, I didn't linger on the thought.

"I don't think the contractors left for River's Edge," I said. "I think they finished the job here."

Leof stood and held out the torch. His eyes turned amber as he reached the same conclusions I did.

Someone intentionally built this awful place.

Krissa strolled from cage to cage. She occasionally reached out and touched the person inside, but moved to the next before they reacted. The prisoners reacted slowly and sluggishly.

"They're still drugging them," I said.

"Probably in the food and water. It keeps them docile."

I wanted to throw up.

Krissa made a noise and fell to her knees beside the last cell in the row.

"Ilene, can you hear me? Are you okay?" She rattled the cage bars.

Ilene didn't move.

"Leof, please, I need you." Krissa's voice was a sob. "Get her out of there."

Leof squeezed my arm as he walked by. I studied the people, all bundled in identical tunics and pants, scanning for Valen's face.

My heart clenched. Nothing. None of them were the man I sought.

Leof's claws scratched against the metal lock. A few prisoners cried out, and more covered their ears. The thick walls created an almost intense silence. Paired with the noise enchantments, they probably didn't hear much besides moaning. The cutting of the lock frightened them.

Krissa pulled Ilene from the cage. She draped herself over Ilene's unmoving form and pressed her ear to the woman's chest. Moments later, Krissa rose and released a tense laugh.

"She's alive. She's okay."

"We need to get all of these people out of here before Elo and Blondie come back." I heard my voice, but my mind only searched for Valen. "Leof, start opening cages." Hopefully, Brew felt my urgency and used the ley-line to get here as soon as possible. I needed the wagon to move all these people to safety.

Leof's claws tore through more locks, and I ventured to the one closest to me. I pulled a pin from my hair and bent it to fit into the keyhole. The interior lock pins pushed against the slim metal as I tried to find the right alignment.

"Rae." My name was small, weak.

I glanced up, slipping the pick from the lock. Damn, I'd have to start over. But Dymetri stared at me through the bars. His face was thin and ashen. They'd cut his hair—more accurately, butchered it —almost to the roots.

I forced a smile. "Fancy seeing you here."

"He said you would come." None of Dy's usual light filled his eyes. "But we didn't believe him."

The lock clicked as I balanced one pin after another into its proper place. Leof probably opened three cages in the time it took me to half-open one.

"The Nightwrath."

The pick slipped again, but I barely noticed. "Valen is here? You've seen him?"

Dy nodded. His head looked too big for his slim neck. "They bring him out as an example of what can happen when we misbehave. Sometimes they leave him here for a while, thinking he's passed out, but that's when he talks about you. His Sunshine."

The nickname stabbed through my heart.

"They hurt him?" I whispered. "Is he . . ." I couldn't force the word out.

Dy nodded, knowing my thoughts. "They always bring a healing tonic. Don't want their best source of information to die. That would be inconvenient."

"What do you mean, their source?" Valen never said anything he didn't want to, and I doubted torture would even change that.

"That's how we're all here. They know there's someone special in Hallow's Promise. They started with Valen to figure out who it is. But he just gives them one name after another, and none of them is yours."

"Valen is giving them false information to protect me?"

Dy licked his lips. His eyes turned glassy. "He's been waiting for you. In the private room . . . at the back . . . We didn't believe him. We . . . should . . . have . . ." The man's words trailed off.

I backed away from the cage. My fingers shook too much to hold the pick, much less work at the lock. Dy was still breathing, only unconscious from the toxins. He would be alright. They all would. Leof and Krissa would get them out and to Brew or somewhere else safe.

I looked for the werewolf. Leof wouldn't let me go to the back room alone, but I didn't want anyone else to see Valen before me.

I approached the wall. Fresh black paint beaded along the rough structure. It had been covered hastily, sloppily. The hidden door was the same color as the wall, and I walked right by it the first time. For the second pass, I ran my fingertips along the edge until the crack pressed against my skin. It didn't have a knob, so I pushed my nails into the groove. My fingertips cried and the nails chipped, but I forced the door open.

Blackness waited for me in the beyond.

I should have gotten Leof. I absolutely should not have gone into the pitch-black secret torture room by myself.

But I grabbed an unlit torch, the piece of flint beside it, stepped inside, and pulled the hidden door closed.

Chapter 26

I was reckless, not stupid. I waited with my back pressed against the door and listened. Nothing moved in the darkness. After a few heartbeats of stillness, I decided it was as safe as a hidden torture room could be. I flicked the flint together and encouraged the sparks to light the oil-soaked torch.

The first fingers of flame light danced over a steep staircase at the very far end of the room. It plunged upward into the ceiling, where a door remained firmly shut at the top. I filled the staircase into the back of my mind as a possible escape route if I needed one.

This room was worse than the other. It was more spacious, but somehow much more terrible than the space full of cages.

One pair of thick chains sprouted from the wall and bound the wrists of a single prisoner, allowing a leeway of two or three feet. His ankles were also shackled, close enough to prevent more than a small shuffle.

It was Valen. It had to be. But I didn't recognize the man on the hard ground. The mercenary was usually larger than life. He made me mad and laugh at the same time. There wasn't anything Valen couldn't do, couldn't overcome.

This man . . .

His hair was shorn close to the scalp, with some new growth

covering the tops of his ears. He was verging on skeletal, obviously not as well fed as the others. Blood, old and new, smudged along his exposed skin, and I suspected more soaked into the fabric of his clothes.

But beneath the twisted appearance, part of him struck a memory at the far back of my mind. Not one of Valen—I barely saw the mercenary I knew in this shell of a person—but of some place also horrific and filled with despair.

I made a noise. The man shifted toward the sound. With a slight groan, he opened his eyes.

It *was* Valen. I saw him now. The blood and the hair couldn't hide those crystal eyes that bore into my soul with an unmatched intensity. My body betrayed all logic. I sprinted to his side, setting the torch down and embracing him with both arms.

"Valen," I whispered, his name every promise I'd ever spoken. "I'm here. I found you."

"Sunshine." His voice cracked. I half-laughed, half-cried. "You're here again."

I ran my finger against his brow. "Again? I just got here."

He laughed, then winced, like something hurt. The shackles rattled, and Valen paused.

"Usually, I'm not all tied up when I dream of you." His gaze sharpened on my face. "And you're not usually injured. Maybe this is it and I'm finally dying."

"Or maybe you're not dreaming."

His eyelids fluttered closed, then sprang back open. "It's always a dream. No matter how real it feels. Just lay with me, Sunshine. Make my last few moments good ones."

"Shut up, Valen. You're not dying. Roll over so I can get these chains off." I tried to move him, but even in his emancipated state, the mercenary refused to budge.

But his gaze sharpened.

"This isn't a dream?" His voice adopted a dangerously low tone.

"I'd like to think your dreams about us don't usually involve a torture dungeon, but to each their own. Move over."

"If this isn't a dream . . ." Valen jerked upright quicker than I expected. A flash of pain pinched his face, but it flattened quickly. "Then, someone actually hurt you." He followed the line of bruising over my cheek, and his gaze darkened. "Who did this to you? I will make sure they'll never hurt you again by removing their head."

"Why does everything keep saying that to me? I hate to break it to you, but you're in no place for revenge beheading at my expense, and also, I can revenge behead my own enemies."

Thumping came from the other side of the wall. Hopefully, it was Leof and Krissa dragging people out, and not them fighting Elo and Blondie.

"Who else is here?" Valen asked as I worked the chains at his wrists. Some kind of magic had been weaved into the metal, which both trapped Valen's power and tickled my fingers as I worked with the pick.

"Who do you think?"

"Probably a marshal and a female civilian. Is that a good guess?"

One shackle popped open.

"You're really good at this guessing game."

The other wrist came free and Valen wrapped me in his arms before I moved onto the leg restraints. He pulled me into his lap and buried his face into my hair.

I sucked in a breath. He smelled awful—like old blood

and bile—but the freshness of forest and spring rain lingered beneath it all. My chest heaved. I didn't want to cry, didn't feel particularly sad as all the adrenaline coursed through my veins, but the sobs came anyway. Valen pushed my head into his shoulder and let me cry.

Everything I'd been working toward was finally in my arms. Valen was alive. He was safe. Maybe not in the best health, but I could fix that.

"I missed you, Sunshine."

"I missed you, too." I wiped the tears from my eyes and pulled back. His face didn't look too bad. He sported bruises beneath both eyes, but I had a black eye, too. But that strange familiarity returned. I squinted and titled my head. The feeling didn't change.

"Sorry I didn't clean up more. I wasn't expecting company."

I laughed. Whatever weird memory hiding at the back of my mind could stay there. I needed to get Valen out.

"Let me work on the leg restraints."

"Don't bother. They're magically reinforced. Only he can open them. We'll have to get out of here, and you can research some fancy science way to remove them."

"He?" I stood and helped Valen to his feet. He swayed but remained standing. I circled my arm around his waist, and we took one slow step after another toward the hidden door in the wall.

"Yeah, did you guys kill him to get in here? I guess not if the shackles are still working . . ."

Valen's weight felt good against my side. We moved slowly, but I savored the contact. "I don't know who he is."

"You know, the sheriff? You must have walked right by him to get in here. He's always playing cards with his two pawns in the front room."

I almost dropped Valen.

"What did you just say?"

He pinched his brow. Obviously, the walking was hard on his battered body because a bead of sweat formed on his forehead. But he didn't complain.

"The sheriff is the one who put all of us in here, Rae. Did you not know that?" He gave a harsh laugh. "Look at that. I solved a case before you for once."

I dragged Valen forward. "I don't think recognizing your kidnapper is the same as solving a case." But my mind spun in circles over the information.

Sheriff Jean orchestrated the kidnapping ring. That's why he didn't care about Pomplo's autopsy. That's how the prison was remodeled without anyone knowing. He'd gone rogue rounding up criminals in Hallow's Promise and storing them in this awful place.

"Why would the sheriff be interested in petty criminals? I mean, they're annoying, but. . . ."

Those blue eyes focused on me. One side of his lips lifted into that tilted smile I loved so much.

"Jean doesn't care about them at all. He's looking for *you*, Rae. He recognized me from Erline and figured out we were both searching for the same thing—the king's lost necromancer."

That didn't make any sense.

"But I never saw you at Erline. I was mostly sequestered from the rest of the king's guests and politicians. Nobody the sheriff knows could have seen me at Erline."

"You weren't sequestered from the prisoners." Valen's voice was soft. A new pain strained his words, and it wasn't physical this time. "At least, not all of them."

"That's true." I tried to recall memories I normally shoved deep, deep into the back of my mind. "I saw the prisoners that the king wanted me to kill."

Valen had stopped walking. I tried to urge him forward, but his gaze was entrapped on my face.

"You also saw the ones he wanted to steal life from."

I pressed my lips together. I never talked about my tasks for the king in Erline. Krissa knew almost all my secrets, and she'd probably figured out what I did with my powers for the king, but I certainly never told Valen.

"How do you know that?" I whispered. I couldn't speak louder. My throat tightened.

The shattered memories I tried to forget realigned painfully. Everything about my past in Erline erupted into the forefront of my thoughts, consuming all else.

I knew what he would say. I knew why his emancipated face and blood-soaked body was so familiar.

"Because I was there, Rae. Because you've met me before."

The memories hurt as they returned.

Blood dripped off the man's sword as I left him in the rain. The stranger had killed every guard standing between me and freedom, and I abandoned him in the downpour. He would be my salvation, to his detriment.

He would die, anyway. Too much power in one body was unsustainable. That's what they told me.

They lied.

"You saved me." The words . . . they couldn't be mine. I was too wrapped in the memories. "You killed them all that night so I could leave."

"Yes. And I've spent every day searching for you since then.

"No. It can't be true . . ."

"It is. All my power comes from you. The Smoke Wielding, traveling by the energy of life, it's all because when you put that power into me, you gave me a piece of yourself. I've always carried your sunshine with me."

I shook my head. There were no excuses for the horror I committed against him. I left him to die, cold and alone, in the rain. "I'm sorry, Valen, for what I did to you . . ."

"Don't be." He wiped the tears from my eyes. "It's the greatest gift I've ever gotten. *You* are the best thing to happen to me."

"I—"

I was interrupted.

"How touching."

Sheriff Jean appeared from behind Valen. Lost in our conversation and my revelations, he'd descended the staircase, and we hadn't noticed.

A twisted smile drew across his lips.

"I'm *so* sorry to interrupt."

And he plunged a sword through Valen's back.

Chapter 27

The little silver tip protruding from Valen's chest didn't look all that intimidating. It lingered there, hesitating a bit as the blade ground against bone, before the sheriff pulled it out. Valen's face slackened. He dropped to his knees, and since I still clung to him, I did too.

Blood fell to the floor in round droplets. They were thick and fat, and there were far too many.

His eyes focused on me. Time wasn't moving quite right, I realized that as I tried to cling to the moments.

A spark inside my chest ignited. The core of my magic awoke. Suddenly, Valen's heartbeat filled my ears.

Tha-thump. Tha-thump. Tha-thump.

He raised a hand to his chest and prodded the wound there. His fingertips stained red.

Tha-thump. Thump.

My magic circled him. It realized that something very powerful was brimming along the horizon.

Valen's hand fell. His face went slack.

Thump. Thump.

Death.

Thump.

Nothing.

The sheriff was talking to me. His words spilled along my empty ears as I cradled Valen's body. His blood poured onto my clothes, encouraged by gravity to flee his cooling body. In a few hours, he'd be icy, then stiff as rigor set in.

My mind detached completely. I recited all the facts I knew about death. Decomposition began immediately as the bacteria inside the gut eagerly consumed the dead organs. Bloating would occur, followed by the purge. Insect activity and maybe those mice Krissa mentioned would consume the flesh until only skeletal material remained. They might even gnaw on the bones for the marrow.

And who would feed Bubbles? Because I wasn't imagining Valen's body succumbing to the awful process of decomposition. I fully planned to curl beside him and experience the same death and decay that he did.

Jean crouched in front of me. He tilted his head.

"You must be in shock, darling. Come on, let's get you something to eat and drink. It's quite the journey back to Erline. I want you in good shape for the king."

He grabbed my upper arm and tried to yank me away. I tightened my grip on Valen's limp body, which proved too heavy for the sheriff to lift.

Valen was dead.

You can bring him back.

My magic whispered in my mind.

For the first time in a long time, I listened to it.

He doesn't have to stay dead. Feed me, and I'll bring him back.

It was my voice, I knew. Magic wasn't a separate entity from the person. It was my subconscious verbalizing the desires of my power. But I listened to the words, encouraged them, and entertained their meaning.

The king would find me. As soon as I used my powers, the king would feel exactly where I was. But the sheriff was ready to drag me back to Erline anyway. If the king found me, I should at least be able to set my terms.

Or, we could kill the sheriff. The king would send a Provider to investigate his death, but Leof and I knew enough about murders and crime to cover it up. I could hide while the Provider poked around, and they would leave, and my secret would be safe forever. The life I'd built, Brew, and all my friends would never encounter the king's wrath.

And Valen would still be dead.

Jean reached for me again but snapped upright as the hidden door along the wall slipped open. He raised his sword, still slick with Valen's blood.

Leof stepped into the room. He glanced at me, with Valen's body across my lap, his blood painting us both. His arms were terrible blends of werewolf claws and human skin. At any other time, the sight would make my stomach clench.

I didn't care much at the moment. I really didn't feel anything at all.

My power swirled around the room again, licking along Valen's skin. It liked the blood-soaked taste and the way it already grayed at the fingertips. It liked whispering in my ear that death was only temporary for us.

Leof must have felt the magic. His gaze turned frantic.

"Rae, listen to me. Don't do it." Leof lowered his voice, trying to be calm. The sheriff paused and glanced between us like he realized something was happening that he didn't understand. "I know it's hard, but you know what the consequences would be. Think about everything you've built. I can't protect you if the king knows where you are."

Every shattered piece in my life aligned in a heartbeat. All the questions I'd pondered since Valen arrived, and Leof made his affections toward me clear. There was only one man that would help me stand on my own feet. Only one man that encouraged *me* to determine right from wrong, not the law or anyone else. There was one man made just for me.

Aw, Leof. His amber eyes were as familiar as my own. I loved him, I really did.

But Valen was *mine*.

I rolled Valen over and stood up. Crimson trailed from his lips. His sightless eyes stared at nothing. The wound across his chest remained hidden beneath his damp clothing.

"Don't worry, darling," the sheriff spoke. Did he know they would be his last words? "Broken hearts heal. And you'll have plenty of time to get over this when you return home to the capital. The king will be very happy to have you back. I can only imagine the rewards he'll give to the devoted citizen who returns you." Jean snapped his sword out toward Leof, disregarding me as threat.

His mistake.

I laughed. The tone sounded too high pitched. A painful echo vibrated from the walls, the ceiling, and shattered back into us. Jean cupped his free hand over his ear, but I reveled in the pain.

"The King of Erline will reward you with your own head on a platter—the same prize he gives to anyone that learns of my existence." Smoke leaked from my sword and swirled around our legs. Jean finally studied me, appraising the threat he carelessly overlooked moments ago. "But you won't have to worry about that, *darling*. I'm happy to complete that task for the king."

"Please, Rae," Leof begged. "Don't do this."

I ignored him. No amount of pleading would change my mind. I refused to live in a world where Valen was dead.

And I didn't have to.

I let my necromancy free. All the power snapped out of me in a rush. I'd forgotten how *good* it felt to use the magic, to feed it. It brushed along the walls, tasted Jean's and Leof's lives. The tiny feet of mice between the bricks. The little flashes of spiders and bugs inside the walls. Everything with any hint of life illuminated within my mind.

But death was brighter.

Valen's body on the ground glowed with ethereal light as my power assessed him. Fresh death carried so much potential. I could awaken his body without the soul, and it would do my bidding. But then he wouldn't call me Sunshine anymore, and where's the fun in that?

So consumed in the freedom of my magic, I barely felt the searing burn on my wrist. If I looked down, the dagger tattoo on my arm would be burning a coal-red color as it alerted the king to my location.

I didn't look down.

Feeling the smoke tendrils was too easy. Their coils bent with my will, wrapping around Jean's legs. He cried out as I anchored him to the floor, and he tried to pull away from the restraints.

"I'm sorry," I mocked him in a sing-song voice. "Don't like the taste of your own medicine?"

He sucked in a breath to scream, but one of the fingers of smoke trapped his mouth shut. No, he deserved to die quietly.

"This isn't you, Rae," Leof whispered.

The werewolf was good in every sense of the word. But he

didn't understand me—not the real me. The rush, the power, the ability to change fate—that was *all* me. It just took this long to figure that out.

"Close your eyes, Leof," I said, gently. I didn't check to see if he listened. That was his choice.

I slammed my power into Jean's body. He screamed against the smoke, the noises consumed into silence. The tendrils of magic pulled apart each string that connected his body to his life. As they freed, I gathered the strings and wove them into a morbid bouquet of power. Jean swayed, then collapsed, then stopped moving completely.

The last of his threads of life snapped into my metaphorical hand. His life was delicious, raw power so sweet in my mind.

I could keep it. The extra power would strengthen my magic. Next time I used it, I would be even more powerful. Unstoppable.

But there was something I wanted more than strength.

I turned to Valen. The smoke wrapped around his body and lifted him into the air toward me. That glow surrounded him.

Carefully, I gathered all the life I'd stolen from Jean and wrapped it around Valen's still form. I took my time, coating him with it until it covered him from head to toe. Once it enveloped him, I carefully pushed the power into his body, reconnecting the severed threads, *willing* him to live.

He had no choice but to obey.

Valen's first breath was ragged and pained. His next loosened as the wounds inside his chest mended. By the third breath, his face had relaxed, and he slept peacefully.

My energy waned. The smoke lowered Valen to the ground, then disappeared. My vision darkened. I hadn't used my power in so long, it felt like a weakened muscle strained from overuse.

I collapsed beside Valen and inched one hand to his chest. His breathing soothed the worry from my mind.

Leof crouched beside us. "You did it."

"Yes," I whispered.

He brushed a strand of hair from my face. I closed my eyes. "The king will send Providers for you."

"Yes."

"I won't let anything happen to you, or anyone else in Hallow's Promise."

"I know." My head hurt. I wanted to curl into Valen's side and sleep forever. "Hallow's Promise needs a new sheriff. Are you up for the job?"

His hand stilled on my forehead. "I guess we won't want one sent from Elrine now."

"Probably not."

Warm lips pressed against my skin. "Consider Hallow's Promise officially severed from Erline's rule. Anything to keep you safe."

I closed my eyes. Sandwiched between Leof and Valen was the safest I could ever be.

Chapter 28

I'd never been to a town meeting before. Usually, I avoided large gatherings of people at all costs, but since I'd sort of caused this one, I decided to attend.

Valen was still weak from his whole rising-from-the-dead ordeal. He hadn't woken yet, but Ilene stayed with him while he recovered on my couch at home. I expected him to wake up anytime, and the thought made my heart speed up.

He must hate me. The words he said in the sheriff's secret dungeon last night were spoken from a place of trauma and tension. Once he realized what I did to him all those years ago, logically, he should flee as far from me as possible.

But illogically, I hoped he didn't.

Elo and Blondie had disappeared. That was my biggest regret from the entire fiasco of the night. Not that the king knew where I was—but that Jean's partners wouldn't answer for their crimes against humanity. I hoped the universe had terrible plans for them.

Leof climbed onto the roughly constructed platform at the intersection near the South Gate. It was the largest place in Hallow's Promise to accommodate the greatest number of people. When he opened his mouth, his voice boomed from the amplification spell I'd cast over him before joining the crowd.

"Last night, Sheriff Jean was murdered in the act of committing a crime." People whispered and covered their mouths. "He had been kidnapping individuals outside the boundaries of the law . . ."

Leof kept talking, but someone touched my hand.

Alivia stood beside me, sheltered in the shadow of the large pine overhead. She wore her typical long cloak, which was unbuttoned today to reveal a silver tunic tucked into leather pants. She'd even abandoned her elbow length gloves, which admittedly, I was thankful for.

"There are rumors stirring in Erline." She didn't quite whisper, but her low tone would prevent most eavesdropping.

"I can imagine what they are."

"The king has gathered his Providers—every last one. Their mission is of the utmost confidentiality."

"So, I'm assuming you know what it is?"

Her gray eyes settled on my face. A whirlpool twisted in their depths, as deep and complicated as the woman they belonged to. "They search for a necromancer the king once lost."

I looked back at Leof on the stage. The sunlight brightened his hair. "I imagine someone like that would try to hide very well."

"Wherever they are hiding, their community has much to thank them for. Afterall, no city has ever split from Erline's rule before now. The kingdom will be watching us. I, for one, am glad to have their attention."

Her fingertips brushed mine again. She turned back into the crowd, and, within a few steps, disappeared completely.

Leof hadn't announced the separation from Erline yet. Alivia's sources were damn good.

"And, if the townsfolk of Hallow's Promise accept me, I will bear the burden of the role of sheriff and lead our city into the new age of independence. Clearly, the rule of Erline tainted the position of our previous sheriff, and that stain cost him his life."

The wolf sucked in a deep breath.

"That is why I am announcing Hallow's Promise as a sovereign territory, uncovered by Erline's laws and leadership. From today on, we dismiss the king's rule and will be governed independently. Anyone who disagrees is free to vacate the city walls as soon as possible. For those that stay, be prepared, for war will not be far behind this announcement."

The whispers ceased. Stillness rippled through the crowd, and I worried they might toss Leof right off the stage.

But someone, somewhere, started clapping.

The applause grew slowly at first, but soon consumed the street in a roaring thunder. The people around me whispered amongst each other about the atrocities Erline had committed against them personally. A cheer erupted near the front of the stage and one young woman reached for Leof's feet and the wolf carefully sidestepped.

Not everyone was happy. A few individuals peeled away from the crowd with their heads down. Some families pulled their children back and hurried along the streets. People would be packing their bags tonight and leaving quickly, for the king did not hesitate to enforce his strict rules.

But mostly, people cheered.

Leof started talking about strategies and tactics, which I interpreted as a good time to leave. He'd come when he needed me.

I certainly wasn't going anywhere.

* * *

Suzie, Krissa, Ilene, Bubbles, and Whiskers huddled around the couch where Valen slept. I worked on the lavender oil in the kitchen, mostly to keep my hands busy. The liquid I'd collected from the stilling process had cooled beautifully, leaving the thick oil resting on top of a layer of water. Separating the oil without contaminating it was a careful process.

Ilene and Krissa held hands. I didn't know where their relationship stood, but Ilene had decided to move her army headquarters to Hallow's Promise since it was separated from Erline. Krissa was thrilled that she'd be around more. I was happy for both of them.

I used a long glass tube to carefully pull out a few drops of oil at a time. I pressed the tube into the liquid until it almost brushed the water layer. Then, I covered the opening of the glass, trapping the lavender inside, and moved it to a smaller jar. It was painstakingly slow.

Krissa gasped. Everyone froze.

"I think he's stirring," she said.

"How? He looks the same as he did ten minutes ago, and ten hours ago before that." Ilene leaned closer to her brother's figure.

"Look at his chest. Watch his breathing."

I kept up my work with the lavender. It wasn't the first time someone decided Valen was about to wake up.

The oil filled the jar one drop at a time. I sucked in the scent. Pure lavender oil was potent but did little to reduce my tension. So much had changed in a single night. Nothing would ever be the same.

A soft moan came from the couch.

I dropped the glass tube so fast that it almost shattered on the countertop, caught by a well-placed dishcloth. I circled the couch, where Valen's fingertips were starting to flutter. We'd cut off his bloodstained clothes and found a clean set. Ilene had carefully wiped the blood from his face and chest, avoiding old and healing wounds.

A dash of blue escaped as his eyelids slightly parted. He blinked twice and moaned once more.

My heart climbed up my throat and tried to spill out of my mouth. Part of me didn't believe he'd really survived—that my magic had saved him. I couldn't deny the truth any longer. He was here.

And he might not want me.

It wasn't all about me, of course. Ilene deserved to have her brother alive. Her rebellion needed his skill set, too. Even if Valen threw me out, which part of me hoped he would, I could never regret giving him life again.

Crystal eyes blinked at the ceiling. I think it took a moment for Valen to recognize the room. His gaze flicked to everyone standing around the couch.

He gave a hint of a smile when he got to Ilene, but it was my face where his sight finally rested.

Valen looked at me for a long time. A knot wrapped inside my chest. I barely breathed while he watched me.

A real smile spread across his lips. When he finally spoke, his voice was quiet, but clear.

"Hello, Sunshine."

* * *

FREE BONUS CHAPTER Sneak Peak

The King of Erline sat up in his bed. The twisted sheets and sweat-soaked blankets revealed what he already knew: he had not slept well. Disease etched along the inside of his body, trying to crawl into his internal organs and smother him. He'd replaced the previous necromancer, but the new one was just as pathetic, neither as powerful as the girl.

Maybe a few days of torture could encourage him to try harder. Yes, the king would send the orders in the morning.

A jolt of pain crawled up his arm. Ah, one of his Providers had used their magic beyond Erline's city walls. That's what woke him......

WANT MORE?

Free BONUS chapter for newsletter subscribers only!
Click the link, visit my website (anpayton.com), or Scan the QR code below:

Want to Support the Author?

The easiest way is to leave a review on your favorite reading platform. Reviews help us get visibility in the community, and spread our books to a wider audience.

Whether or not you choose to leave a review, THANK YOU for being here and reading our books.

Acknowledgments

As always, a surplus of credit goes to Nicole at The Assist, LLC! She sees these drafts in their raw, ugly form and doesn't run away screaming (at least, not that she tells me).

Thank you to GetCovers for another round of cover design and edits.

A specific thank you to my Mother-In-Law. I hope you know that the part where they're discussing the size of men's . . . weapons - they mean swords. I promise. (*secret wink*).

My husband and kiddos can't get a pass - they're truly my biggest fans. In fact, there's book art hanging on the wall that I never would have put up. It makes my day better knowing you're all in it.

And, especially, every time, **THANK YOU** to all my readers. Without you, Hallow's Promise is simply a hallucination in my head. I hope you continue reading, so I can stay out of an institution. Until the next one, cheers.

About the Author

A.N. Payton is a fantasy romance author, true-crime obsessee, and a very low-skilled seamstress. She writes at the inter-section of fantasy and science, with a dash (or overflowing scoop) of romance. Her books are concocted with the perfect proportions of strong female characters, sexy men who may or may not end up shirtless, and plenty of sarcastic banter.

A.N. Payton spends her days at a top-secret job (if she told you, she'd have to kill you), which proves real life is more wild than fiction. At night she escapes by writing new worlds and problems for someone else to solve - probably with a sword.

She lives in the pacific northwest with a husband she loves (depending on the day), two kids she loves (most of the time), and a dog she loves (all the time).

Other Works by A.N. Payton

Princess Sal's magic bought her people peace and security, but she'll never be safe with the vampire king in her castle.

Centuries of war come to a bitter end when Princess Sal's parents steal half the witch army and disappear. Sal is forced to surrender to the vampire king, Kadence, and bind her magic as part of their agreement. She will give anything to protect her people – anything except her heart.

When Kadence conquers the witch kingdom, he doesn't expect their princess to be as delicious as wild honey. He can't decide if he'd rather kiss or kill Sal, and his desire for her battles against his hatred of witches. Despite their attraction, Kadence can't forget their war-torn history. He must decide if he can overcome his past to make way for a new future – one that might include Sal.

But when scouts locate Sal's parents and discover they're marching a demon army toward the kingdom, Sal and Kadence must unite their people for a final battle. If they don't, bloodthirsty demons will consume everyone they vowed to protect. Can they work together to save their people, or will hellfire destroy them all?

187